YOUNG JANE CANFIELD goes to spend the summer in the large, dark mansion of her grandmother in Lynn, Massachusetts. From the first, she feels the presence of Emily, the long-dead daughter of Mrs. Canfield. Louisa, Jane's eighteen-year-old aunt and companion, believes that Jane's relationship with the dead and dark-eyed Emily is only the product of a lonely child's imagination. But the evil force becomes too strong and soon Jane is fighting for her life.

PATRICIA CLAPP comes from the New England of Jane and Emily. She has also written CONSTANCE: A STORY OF EARLY PLYMOUTH. Aside from being a grandmother of nine, she is kept busy as a playwright, a librarian for the New Jersey Theatre League, and a director of the Studio Playhouse of Essex County, N. J.

LAUREL-LEAF BOOKS bring together under a single imprint outstanding works of fiction and nonfiction particularly suitable for young adult readers, both in and out of the classroom. Charles F. Reasoner, Professor of Elementary Education, New York University, is consultant to this series.

# ❧ *Jane-Emily* ❧

## A NOVEL BY

## Patricia Clapp

Published by
Dell Publishing Co., Inc.
1 Dag Hammarskjold Plaza
New York, New York 10017
Copyright © 1969 by Patricia Clapp
All rights reserved.
For information, address Lothrop, Lee & Shepard Co.
Laurel-Leaf Library ® TM 766734,
Dell Publishing Co., Inc.

ISBN: 0-440-94185-7

RL: 5.1

Reprinted by arrangement with Lothrop,
Lee & Shepard Co., New York
Printed in the United States of America
First Laurel printing—August 1971
Second Laurel printing—October 1971
Third Laurel printing—January 1972
Fourth Laurel printing—May 1972
Fifth Laurel printing—September 1972
Sixth Laurel printing—October 1972
Seventh Laurel printing—April 1973
Eighth Laurel printing—July 1973
Ninth Laurel printing—September 1978
Tenth Laurel printing—October 1980

This book is dedicated
to the memories of those people
for whom it comes too late,
Elizabeth and Howard,
and Ethel and Grandmère

# Jane-Emily

# ONE

There are times when the midsummer sun strikes cold, and when the leaping flames of a hearthfire give no heat. Times when the chill within us comes not from fears we know, but from fears unknown —and forever unknowable.

But on that sunny June afternoon when Jane and I first arrived at her grandmother's house in Lynn, my greatest fear was that I should be overcome by loneliness and boredom before the summer was done. The year was 1912, I was just eighteen, and the thought of leaving Martin Driscoll and being cooped up for the shining vacation months with elderly and quite awe-inspiring Mrs. Canfield, with the almost equally elderly, if more friendly, maid, Katie, and with my niece, nine-year-old Jane Canfield, was less than appealing.

Jane had been orphaned the year before when her mother, my elder sister Charlotte, and her father, Mrs. Canfield's son John, were killed. They had been driving their quiet old horse hitched to the buggy, for even though many people have automobiles now, Charlotte still liked the gentle pace of horse travel better than the dust and noise of motor cars. No one has ever been able to understand what the horse shied at, what frightened him so that he must have reared and turned, tip-

ping the buggy and throwing Charlotte so hard
against a great tree trunk that she died instantly.
John, grasping the reins and striving to control
the animal, was dragged quite horribly for some
distance. No one saw it happen, and John never
regained consciousness, so the cause of the accident has always been a mystery.

My mother and father, Martha and Charles
Amory, took Jane, and gave her warmth and love
and security, but Jane was still unnaturally with-
drawn. She was bright and well-mannered and
sweet, but she rarely laughed and I never saw her
really *play*. She read, or sketched—she was quite
gifted with her pencil—or just sat dreaming into
space. I was very fond of Jane, and I tried to interest her in other things, such as the dolls
Charlotte and I used to play with, or my bicycle,
or any of the other oddments that remained around
the house, but nothing roused more than a polite
interest.

When Lydia Canfield wrote Mother, suggesting
that Jane spend the summer with her, it was felt
the change might do her good—take her out of
herself a bit. I backed the idea enthusiastically
until I learned that Mrs. Canfield seemed reluctant
to assume the care of the child, even with Katie's
help, and had suggested that I accompany her.

"But why me?" I wailed to Mother. "Jane's not a
baby. She can look out for herself."

"Yes, I'm sure she can," Mother agreed. "But
Lydia Canfield isn't used to young children and I
certainly don't want her to spend the summer fret-
ting. You could do a great many things for Jane
that her grandmother might not know how to do."

"But *Mother!* Martin and I have a million plans
for this summer! He's going to read Shakespeare

out loud to me, and I'm going to teach him to play tennis. Besides, what could I do for Jane?"

"Braid her hair, and—"

"I don't see why I should give up a whole summer with Martin just to braid Jane's hair! He'll be going to college in September and I won't have seen him at *all!*"

"Louisa, you have seen enough of Martin Driscoll during the past six months to last for the next six years!"

"You don't like Martin. I know you don't."

"I don't dislike him. He's a perfectly nice boy. But it wouldn't do you any harm to meet some other young men."

"I'm not very likely to meet *anyone* locked up in that gloomy old cave in Lynn!"

But I knew it was a losing battle. Charlotte and I were raised in the school of strict obedience and when we were told, or even asked, to do something, we did it.

"It's going to be absolutely awful!" I muttered, "Martin will forget all about me and I won't meet another living soul and I'll probably end up an old maid!"

Mother laughed and hugged me. "That's extremely unlikely," she said. "And just remember, darling, if you and Jane are both miserable we can always cut the visit short."

How many times later I looked back, remembering those words. If I had forced myself to leave, if I had gone home and taken Jane with me, if we *had* "cut the visit short," would things have been different? Or would that last rainy night always have been waiting somewhere to happen? But at the time all I knew was that we were thirty miles from home, embarked on a summer which, while it might not be truly dismal, certainly promised no great diversion.

However, it always seems to me easier to be happy than unhappy, and since there I was, and there I was going to stay, it was only intelligent to find whatever pleasant aspects there might be in the months ahead. There would, for example, be letters from Martin, and these I looked forward to eagerly. The last evening, when he had come to say good-bye, we had sat in the porch hammock, his arm around my waist and my head on his shoulder, and he had promised to write every day.

"And you must only read the letters when you are alone, Louisa. When you can't be interrupted. Because I shall be writing my deepest thoughts, and you must read them just as you listen to me now. With your whole attention."

My eyes had misted as I promised. Martin's deepest thoughts were very beautiful.

"And you will write to *me* every day, Louisa?"

"Well, I'll try, Martin. But I may be busy sometimes—looking out for Jane, and everything. I may not be able to write *every* day." Somehow I could not bring myself to admit that I detested writing letters, and that they always came out sounding stiff and stupid.

Later, when we heard Father start to cough and clear his throat, the sound coming just as clearly as he intended it to through the open window, Martin kissed me good-bye quite passionately. When he left I stood at the top of the porch steps and waved as long as I could see him in the faint starlight, and then went into the house, my eyes filled with tears.

But the train trip, the first I had ever taken without my parents, was exciting, and somehow by the time Jane and I arrived in Lynn I was not as despondent as I had expected to be.

Jane and I had connecting rooms at the back of the big Canfield house, overlooking the garden. Large and square, each room had high, narrow windows framed in heavy drapes, looped back with thick silk cords. The June sunshine came through my two windows now, falling in bright pools on the rose-patterned carpet. The windows were closed—in fact the whole house had an air of being closed—but I managed to raise both lower panes as far as they would go, delighting in the smell and freshness that drifted in.

"Jane," I called through the open doorway. "Are your windows open? Shall I raise them for you? They're quite stiff."

There was no answer, and I went to the door that led to Jane's room. She was standing by the closed window, her forehead against the glass, gazing out into the garden.

"Jane," I said again. "Don't you want the windows open? The air is wonderful!"

Jane turned slowly and looked at me. "What? I'm sorry. I wasn't listening. Isn't the garden beautiful?"

With affectionate exasperation I moved her so that I could lift the sash. "It's lovely. Here, smell! Isn't that better?"

"Thank you, Louisa."

"Get your bags unpacked and put some of your things away, then you can go out. I'll finish up for you."

With the first real enthusiasm I had seen Jane show in months she went quickly to the luggage rack at the foot of her bed where her valise lay open, and started taking her crisp summer dresses

from it and hanging them in the tall wardrobe
that filled one corner of the room. The rod was so
high that she hopped up on a small two-step
contrivance which stood in position by the wardrobe door.

"Your grandmother is well prepared for you,
isn't she?" I said. "She must have known the rod
would be too high for you to reach."

"This was made for Emily," Jane said. "This was
her room."

"Emily?"

"My father's sister. She died, you know. Years
ago, when she was just twelve."

"Oh. Yes, I think I do recall hearing your mother
speak of her. I had forgotten. How very sad that
she died when she was so young."

"I suppose it is," Jane said with that cool im-
personality that children have for people they
never knew. "Louisa, that's all my dresses. Can't
I leave the rest until later? Nothing else will
wrinkle."

"All right, go along. I'll be down soon."

"Thank you," said Jane, and was out the door
into the hall in a flash. I heard her feet thudding
down the carpeted stairs. A moment later a screen
door slammed somewhere and then I saw her
running across the yard, the sun shining on her
long dark braids. She went straight as an arrow
to a large bright reflecting ball which stood on its
stone pedestal in the exact center of the garden,
and I smiled as I remembered the amusingly
distorted images that one could see in such silver
globes.

Turning back to complete the unpacking, I
thought that in spite of *my* feelings about it, this
summer might truly be good for Jane. She al-

ready seemed happier and more at ease than I had seen her since her mother and father died.

It was close to an hour later before I had emptied the suitcases, put Jane's and my clothes neatly away, washed the train dust from my hands and face, changed out of my traveling suit, and straightened my hair. I inspected myself carefully in the tall mirror to be sure I looked neat enough to win Mrs. Canfield's approval; although I had seen her but rarely, I suspected she was not the sort of woman to tolerate laxity in dress or behavior.

My blond hair, too pale, and inclined to be overly curly, I had managed to brush successfully into a soft roll around my head, twisting the back into a thick knot. I moistened a finger with my tongue and smoothed my brows, accenting their brown arch, and brushing my lashes—which are very thick, as my hair is, but not as pale. My eyes are just plain blue, except that Martin once told me they turn green when I am angry.

The dress I had put on was a lilac voile, held snugly at the waist by a deeper violet sash, and it fell to my ankles. I felt that I looked quite presentable; and hoping fervently that I could live up to the outer image, I made my way through the long, carpeted corridor, down the wide angular staircase to the lower hall, across the dim parlor and out through one of the tall French doors that led to the garden.

Mrs. Canfield sat in one of several wicker chairs placed in the shade of a wide-branching tulip tree. She looked so straight and formal that I found myself walking decorously across the velvet grass to join her. As I approached she looked up and smiled.

"Ah, Louisa. How fresh you look, child! Sit here in the shade and tell me about your parents. They are well, I trust?"

"Quite well, thank you. They asked me to give you their very warmest greetings."

"How kind of them. And your trip was not too unpleasant?"

"Not at all. Both Jane and I enjoyed it."

"Perhaps a cup of tea would be refreshing. I have asked Katie to bring it out here."

"Thank you," I said. Mrs. Canfield made me feel ill at ease and unnaturally prim. Even my words sounded stiff. "How beautiful it is here! I don't wonder that Jane was so happy to come."

"Was she happy? How nice! Of course she was here often before—before the accident, but I did not know whether she would want to come back. It cannot be much entertainment for her, I'm afraid." She leaned forward slightly and laid her small hand on my arm. "I am most grateful to you, my dear, for consenting to spend the summer with her."

"I was glad to," I said, trusting that this was what might be called a "white fib."

I looked across the garden to where Jane was walking slowly up and down the bright rows of flowers, her hands clasped behind her back, seeming to examine each brilliant bloom.

"I love Jane so much, but I wish she was—well, not so *inside* herself. She doesn't laugh, or run, or play the way a little girl ought to. She's—she's too quiet!"

"I shall ask Katie to help me search out some of Emily's old toys," Mrs. Canfield said. "They are all packed away in the attic, and there might be something among them that would amuse Jane."

"I can help, if you like," I offered.

"That would be very kind of you, Louisa."

Involuntarily I glanced up at the house. It stood tall and dark gray, with gables and half-hidden dormers, its several brick chimneys soot-stained almost to black. In most of the rear windows the shades were drawn halfway down, rather like heavy-lidded eyes. Only the four windows on the second floor which were Jane's and mine stood wide open with the shades raised to the top, and two on the first floor in what I judged would be the kitchen. At least Katie believes in letting in a little air, I thought, but the attic probably hasn't seen a ray of sunshine in years. Strangely, I shivered a little and turned back to the lovely yard in which we sat.

As warm and lush and fragrant as it was, the garden had a certain strict control about it. The heavy-headed summer flowers grew neatly within their bounds, the tidy hedges of boxwood and privet were trimmed and even, the thick soft grass was perfectly cut and disciplined. But the rich scent of stock and viburnum drifted lazily on the air, birdcalls lilted from the top of the tulip tree, and bright rows of pansies marched along the sharply-edged borders, their gay faces lending a flippancy to the dignity of the place.

I felt the garden was much like Lydia Canfield herself. Restrained, calm, precise, yet with a natural force and energy which must require a constant effort to hold it always in control. She had been born and bred a Bostonian, I knew, and had not moved to Lynn until the early years of her marriage. She was small, slim, determinedly erect, and I had never seen her dressed in anything other than black taffeta, her chin held high by a boned

lace collar. Her hair, gleaming now blue-black in
the sun, was just beginning to show bright silver
threads in the intricate coronet of braids. She
always wore the same four pieces of jewelry: her
wide gold wedding band, two magnificent diamond
rings, and a long jet chain from which hung an
oval black locket, its smooth surface highlighted
by another large diamond. She had what Jane
called a "closed-up face," and although her voice
was low and beautifully modulated, it lacked
warmth. Somehow, through her cool reserve, she
gave off an air of strength which was impressive.
I was not exactly afraid of Lydia Canfield, but I
was quite awed by her, and very much on my best
behavior.

I heard the back screen door open and close,
and turning, saw Katie coming across the yard
with the tea tray. She set it on a low table by Mrs.
Canfield's chair.

"I made sugar cookies for Jane," she said, "and
there's milk for her in the little pitcher."

"You'll spoil her, Katie," I said lightly.

"Nonsense, Miss Louisa! She could use a mite of
spoiling, seems to me. It doesn't set right to see a
child so quiet." She turned to Mrs. Canfield. "Shall
I fetch her, ma'am?"

"Please, Katie."

Her ample body in its neat gray uniform looked
solid and dependable as she walked across the
grass toward where Jane knelt by a pansy bed.

"Dear Katie," Mrs. Canfield murmured with a
little smile. "Nothing could make her happier than
having a child around to cater to. If we don't watch
her she'll stuff Jane as full of goodies as a Christ-
mas pudding."

"Has Katie been with you long?" I asked.

"Since I was married. She was only sixteen then, inexperienced, but quite desperately anxious to learn. Katie and I have been together for almost forty years. A very long time."

"She knew John, then."

"Oh, yes. From the time he was born. John was always so very fond of Katie!"

"And Emily, too?" I asked.

"Emily?" The barest suggestion of a frown touched her brow and was gone. "Emily was . . . rather different. She demanded a great deal, even from Katie."

"From the little I have seen of Katie I imagine she would enjoy putting herself out for any child."

"Katie is very fond of all children, fortunately. She has always had infinite patience with them. Even with Emily."

I could not help probing. "Even?" I repeated.

"Emily was . . . not particularly considerate of other people."

It seemed a surprising statement for a mother to make, and it embarrassed me a little.

"I suppose all children are a little selfish about their own interests," I said.

"No, not all," Mrs. Canfield replied. Then she lowered her eyes and leaning forward, lifted the silver teapot. "How do you like your tea, my dear?" she asked.

"Sugar, please. And lemon."

As the clear amber fluid flowed smoothly into the delicate cups I watched her face, puzzled by what she had said, and looking for some explanation. But the "closed-up" look was there and I felt unable to pursue the subject. Mrs. Canfield added sugar to my tea, and a thin slice of lemon studded with a clove, handing it to me just as Jane came across the grass toward us, and Katie went back into the house.

"Jane, dear," Mrs. Canfield said. "Did Katie tell you she made cookies for you? And here is your milk."

"Yes. She told me. May I have two?"

"If you like."

Jane chose one of the deeper chairs, pulling her legs under her and sitting comfortably curled while she nibbled round and round the edge of her cookie, her dark eyes full of quiet pleasure.

"Isn't it nice here, Louisa?" she said at last. "I told you it was. I said you would like it. Remember?"

"I do. And you were quite right."

"Even though I know you didn't want to leave Martin," she added.

"Oh—Martin," I said weakly, wishing Jane wouldn't be so outspoken.

Mrs. Canfield looked at me with polite interest. "Martin? He is your . . . beau?"

"Not exactly. At least, not yet."

"I think he is," Jane offered. "He's there at our house practically every minute. And he always wishes I wasn't around."

"Jane!" I had a strong desire to tell my niece to be quiet, but I didn't quite dare. "Martin is very fond of you."

"Oh, he likes me all right, but he still wishes I wasn't around." She turned to her grandmother. "He writes poetry about Louisa, and he can't read it to her when I'm there."

I could feel myself flushing with annoyance and embarrassment. To my relief Mrs. Canfield deftly turned the conversation.

"He must be very clever to write poetry," she

said. "It is something I have never been able to do. Emily used to, however. Have you ever tried, Jane?"

"To write a poem? No, but I don't think it can be so very hard. Did Emily write good poetry? I mean, did it rhyme and everything?"

"Yes, it was quite good, as a matter of fact. I have a copybook somewhere in which she kept them. Perhaps I can find it for you. She wrote a very nice one about pansies once, I recall."

"I like the pansies," Jane said. "Will you come and look at them when you're done with your tea, Louisa? Some of them are enormous!"

"Perhaps."

"They look like tiny little people," Jane mused. "They all have faces, just like tiny people."

"That is what your Aunt Emily used to call them," Mrs. Canfield said. "Her pansy people. She would pick one and say that was the king, and another one would be the queen, and others were their subjects."

Jane looked up at her grandmother. "You mean she really picked them? Or she just *chose* them?"

"She picked them. She had a sandbox, I remember, and she used to stick the stems into the sand so the flowers would stand up."

There was deep concern in Jane's voice. "But didn't they die? With no water, didn't they die?"

"Why, yes," Mrs. Canfield said, "I fancy they did. But by then she was through playing with them."

"I wouldn't want them to die," Jane said positively. "I wouldn't pick them unless I was going to put them in water."

I set my empty cup on the tray and wiped my lips with my napkin. Jane looked so troubled that

I could not remain put out by her remarks about Martin. Besides, he *did* write poetry, and he *didn't* like her around when he wanted to read it to me.

"Jane, everyone picks flowers," I said, "that's why people have gardens. And pansies grow better the more you pick them."

"It's all right if you're going to put them in water," Jane said. "But you should never make anything die!"

She swallowed the last bite of the second cookie, finished off her milk, and wiped her mouth on the back of her hand.

"Jane!" I started to remonstrate. "Use your napkin—"

"Let her be, Louisa," Mrs. Canfield said surprisingly. "Perhaps we fret too much about manners. There is plenty of time for those. For a little while let us both help her to enjoy herself." She gazed at Jane, and her eyes were brooding. "Time is so short—it goes so swiftly—"

I rose. "Jane, will you show me the pansies now?"

Jane bounced from her chair. "This way," she said, and pulled on my hand. "Come on, Louisa, *run!*"

Delighted at being freed from that formal tea table, I picked up my skirts and raced Jane across the grass. Beside me she laughed exultantly.

# TWO

The soft summer days flowed by. Letters from Martin arrived regularly and they were the only thing that broke the unchanging rhythm of routine. I would take them to my room to read in private as I had promised to do, and open each one eagerly. Martin's handwriting was quite large and sprawly and what felt at first like a very thick and rewarding letter often turned out to be no more than a few lines scattered over several pages. But the lines were often poetry, which made me feel very special, and reading about the beauty of my hair or my eyes or my "rose-tipped" hands was flattering, to say the least. The letters made me miss him, and I longed to be home again where I could hear his light voice saying these sweet things to me, rather than having to decipher them from the written page.

Answering his letters was difficult, however, and mine were generally rambling accounts of uneventful days, spiced with a mention of my latest trip to the library or the progress of the campanula plants in the garden. I could have written a great deal about Jane, but I doubted that Martin would be interested in the fact that she was happier than in months.

She seemed to be lowering the wall she had

built around herself, making herself more open to new experiences, more willing to be the warm, friendly child she had been before her parents died. In a sense I suppose she was making herself more vulnerable too, more easily hurt or frightened, but how could I know there could be anything in that quiet Lynn household to hurt or frighten her?

She spent almost all her waking hours in the garden and seemed content to play her own private games with the flowers, to follow Jacob, the weekly gardener, watching him weed and trim and rake. She tried her hand at pushing the lawn mower and was delighted when she could cut a clean straight path in the emerald grass.

Most of all she was fascinated by the reflecting ball.

"It used to be Emily's," she told me. "Emily wouldn't let anyone else look in it. *Ever!*"

"How do you know that?"

"Katie told me. Katie thinks it's marked with evil."

"Jane! What a thing to say!"

"I didn't say it, Katie did. Katie says no good ever came from anything that doesn't show the truth."

"And doesn't the reflecting ball show the truth?"

We were in the garden, and I was trying lackadaisically to write a letter to Martin. Jane went close to the silver ball, putting her face down near it.

"I guess not," she said, and giggled, a lovely sound. "I look like a frog, and I *know* I'm not a frog. But I have a flat nose, and bulgy eyes, and a big wide mouth!"

She stood staring into the silvery surface, making ridiculous faces and giggling at the reflection. "I can look like a lot of different people," she said. She puffed out her rosy cheeks. "Now I look like Queen Victoria!"

I laughed at her. "How do you know what Queen Victoria looked like?"

"I've seen pictures, of course." She opened her eyes wide and tipped her head down slightly, looking upward into the ball through her dark lashes. "Now I look like Emily."

"Where did you see a picture of Emily?" I asked lazily. I could feel the sun warm on my head, and I felt pleasantly drowsy. After a moment I realized Jane had not answered. "Where did you see Emily's picture?" I repeated.

Jane stepped backward, away from the ball, her face very still. "I never did," she said softly.

"You must have, else how would you know you looked like her?"

"I never did," she said again, and suddenly her voice was angry. "I never saw a picture of Emily! But I looked like her! I know I did!" She came quickly to my chair, standing close beside it, her eyes stormy.

"Well, all right, dear," I said in surprise. "As you told me, you can look like all sorts of people in the ball. Queen Victoria, and a frog—why not Emily, too?" I put my unfinished letter and box of writing materials aside. "Let's see who I look like, shall we? Maybe I can be President Taft!"

"No! I don't want you to, Louisa. Anyway, you're just being silly about it! You couldn't look *anything* like President Taft, and I *did* look like Emily! So there!"

She stood a moment, her face flushed and her breath coming quickly. Then she buried her face in my shoulder, hugging me tight.

"I'm sorry, Louisa. I'm sorry! I don't know why I—I didn,t mean to talk like that!"

She sounded deeply disturbed, and it puzzled me, but I thought it probably better to drop the whole subject.

I wondered once or twice about that odd little scene, and I hoped that being at the Canfield house would not create any morbid thoughts in Jane's mind. After all, it had been her father's home, and he was dead; her Aunt Emily had lived here and had died; Mr. Canfield, too, although I could not recall ever having heard much about him. I only knew that he had died before John and Charlotte were married, as had Emily, of course. But in the days that followed I put it out of my mind. There was no further reference to Emily, and I began to think I had imagined the whole incident.

It was at breakfast a week or so later that Mrs. Canfield looked up over a letter she was reading.

"Oh, how nice!" she said. "Adam is back! He asks to come and call."

I slipped my own letter from Martin into my lap to be savored later. Having no idea at all who Adam was, I tried to look interested. It was Jane who asked, "Adam who?"

"Forgive me," Mrs. Canfield said. "Of course you don't know him at all, do you? Adam Frost. He is Dr. Frost now, and he is back in town to work with his father. I suppose it will be Old Dr. Frost and Young Dr. Frost, won't it? How pleasant it will be to see him again!"

"Was he a friend of my father's?"

"Not a close friend. He and Emily were constant playmates from the time they were very small. Adam's mother was a dear friend of mine, and we often spent afternoons together with our children. After Mrs. Frost died Adam still came here frequently. I often thought it must have been simply from habit, because he and Emily had some memorable battles! They were the same age—that would make Adam twenty-four now. Quite young to have completed his medical training."

Jane swirled brown sugar artistically into her porridge. "I don't think twenty-four is so young," she said.

Lydia Canfield smiled at her. "No, I suppose not. But I assure you, it is." Turning to me, she went on, "Adam was always a brilliant boy. Not really a *genius*, I guess, but certainly very, very bright. He was a challenge to Emily. I remember she used to say she was going to marry him when she grew up."

Jane looked up from her cereal. "Did he want to marry Emily?"

"I don't expect she ever gave him a chance to say. It would not have been like her. She was used to announcing her wishes and having them obeyed."

"Did you do everything she wanted you to, Grandmother?" Jane asked with interest.

Mrs. Canfield looked at her thoughtfully. "Far more often than I should have, I fancy," she said. Then she reached over and patted Jane's hand. "But don't get your hopes up, child. I have learned a great deal since then."

"Well, *I* think it was silly of Emily to talk about getting married," Jane said, licking the last cream from her spoon. "I don't intend to think about getting married for years and years and years. Maybe never!" Folding her napkin, she slipped it into the heavy silver ring. "Excuse me, please, Grandmother."

Jane skipped out the swinging door, and we could hear her chattering to Katie in the kitchen. Mrs. Canfield looked down at Dr. Frost's letter again, as I clasped mine from Martin.

"I shall ask Adam to have supper with us on Sunday," she said. "I'm sure you will find him excellent company, Louisa."

"I am sure I shall," I agreed, but a doctor who was almost a genius sounded rather forbidding.

On Sunday when the noon meal was done Mrs. Canfield excused herself to lie down for a while, and Jane and I wandered into the garden.

"Oof, I'm full!" Jane remarked inelegantly, stretching out on her back on the grass.

"I'm not surprised. I counted the helpings of strawberry shortcake you had."

Jane grinned at me. "It was good." She patted her stomach. "I bet I'm getting fat. When we go home I'll probably be as fat as a pig. Granny Amory won't even know me."

"She will be pleased, though." I hesitated, and then added, "Will you hate to leave here when it is time to go?"

Jane pulled up a blade of grass and bit the tender end. "I don't know. I don't think so. I like it here, but it's really Emily's house. Not mine."

"Why, Jane," I said in surprise, "how silly! It's as much yours as hers. It was your father's house, too."

"I know. But it doesn't feel like his. It only feels like Emily's. And Grandmother's, of course."

"You think a lot about Emily, don't you?" I asked.

"Emily thinks a lot about me."

"Jane, don't be ridiculous! You're imagining things. Emily died years ago, long before you were even born."

"I know she did."

"Then don't you see—it's nonsense to say she thinks about you."

"She does, though. I feel her, a lot of times."

"Jane, don't talk like that! You can't 'feel' Emily. Emily isn't anything anymore—except a memory to the people who knew her. Just the memory of a poor little girl who died before she ever had a chance to grow up. And don't keep thinking so much about her! It isn't . . . well, it isn't *healthy*, Jane!"

"Don't worry, Louisa. I'm perfectly healthy. You just said I was getting fat."

I felt suddenly edgy and a little out of patience with her. "I don't mean that kind of healthy!"

Jane laid one little brown hand on my knee. "Don't worry, Louisa. Emily doesn't go skittering around the garden like a white cloud, and she doesn't make funny noises in the night, or anything scary like that. She's just *here*. And she knows I'm here, too. But she hasn't spoken to me yet."

"Well, you just tell me when she does," I said tartly, "because that's the day I'll give you a large dose of castor oil and put you to bed for a week! With *no* strawberry shortcake!"

Jane laughed. "You're funny, Louisa," she said. "I love you. I'm glad I have you."

"Well, if you really love me, stop talking nonsense," I said, but I couldn't help smiling at her.

Flopping over onto her stomach, her two feet

waving in the air, she asked, "What are you going to wear tonight?"

"Tonight? Why, what I have on, I suppose. Should I be changing for some reason?"

She looked at me, amazed. "Dr. Frost is coming to supper! Didn't you remember? Wear your white dress, Louisa, with the blue sash. Please, will you? You haven't worn it since you've been here, and it's the prettiest of all your dresses."

"Why should I get all dressed up just because a friend of your grandmother's is coming to see her?"

"He's not too old for you. Maybe he'll fall in love with you."

"Why, naturally he will! How could he help it? He will walk into the parlor, take one look at me and throw himself flat on his face at my feet. Oh, Jane, you *are* a goose!"

"Is Martin in love with you?"

As a straight question I found it a little difficult to answer. "Why, I don't exactly know. I guess he is—sort of."

"Are you going to marry him?"

"Maybe. Someday. When he's through college."

"Dr. Frost is already through college. You wouldn't have to wait."

"Jane, would you mind very much letting me run my own life?"

"I only mentioned it. *I* think Martin's soppy!"

"Well, *I* like him very much! And I wish *he* was coming to supper instead of the brilliant Dr. Whatshisname!"

"Won't you even *talk* to him, Louisa?"

"To whom?"

"Brilliant Dr. Whatshisname."

I picked up my box of writing materials and laid

it on my lap. "I'm sure I can find something to say to him," I replied. "Perhaps he'd like to hear about my tonsil operation. Now if you will very kindly be quiet, I am going to write to Martin!"

Jane got lazily to her feet and slipped her hand in mine, her mouth turning up in its own appealing way. "Wear the white dress anyhow, Louisa, will you? Please? Just for me."

It was a few minutes before six that evening, and I was just tying small pink bows on Jane's braids when we heard the sharp jangle of the doorbell.

"Oh, Louisa, he's here! Hurry!"

"Stand still! I can't tie bows when you wiggle! There. Now, let me look at you."

Her pink dotted swiss dress was fresh from Katie's skillful iron, her long white ribbed cotton stockings were smooth, and her black patent leather slippers gleamed from the trace of Vaseline I had rubbed into them.

"All right, go ahead. I'll be down in a minute or two." She bounced toward the door, her braids swinging. "And Jane! Walk! Like a lady! Don't go crashing down the stairs!"

She made me a mock curtsy. "Yes, ma'am," she said, and went mincing along the hall with exaggerated daintiness.

After a moment's hesitation I lifted the white dress from its hanger, and put it carefully over my head. The soft muslin felt light and cool as the skirt, with its dozens of tiny tucks, slipped easily over the starched petticoat. The neck was wide and square, edged with a lace ruffle, and wider ruffles fell from the short sleeves. The pale blue

taffeta sash was crushed and fitted tight to my
waist, making it look extremely small. I clipped
flat blue bows onto my white slippers, tucked another into my hair, and took a careful look in the
mirror. I couldn't help being satisfied with what
I saw.

"Well, Dr. Whatshisname," I murmured, "here
comes the irresistible Louisa Amory!"

There were voices from the parlor, and not
wanting to interrupt a conversation, I paused by
the open door. Mrs. Canfield sat in the small wing
chair that she always preferred, and Jane was
curled on a deep red velvet ottoman close beside
her. Both their faces were smiling and lifted
toward the man who stood talking, his back to
the door. Beside the two small seated figures he
seemed very tall. His head was narrow and well-
shaped, his hair thick and dark and closely
cropped, probably in an effort to discourage its
definite tendency to curl. He stood easily, one
hand in the pocket of his gray jacket, the other
holding a pipe with which he gestured.

Lydia Canfield saw me in the doorway and held
out her hand. "Come in, child. Adam, this is
Louisa Amory, Jane's aunt."

He was quite nice-looking, with flat planes to
his cheeks and jaw, and a sort of cleft in his chin.
I remembered a silly rhyme Mother sometimes
quoted. "Cleft in the chin, devil within," but this
doctor looked anything but devilish.

"Miss Amory," he said. "I have wanted so much
to meet you!"

Since he probably hadn't known I existed until
five minutes before, I was inclined to doubt this
remark.

"And I have been looking forward to meeting you, Dr. Frost. Mrs. Canfield speaks so highly of you."

I extended my hand and he took it. "Mrs. Canfield is prejudiced in my favor," he said rather pompously, "but I have no desire to change her opinion."

As I removed my hand from his and sat down, Jane said with suspicious innocence, "Dr. Frost, do you write poetry?"

The man looked at her in astonishment. "Poetry? Good heavens, no! Why?"

Jane smiled sweetly. "I just wondered. I think men who write poetry are kind of soppy, don't you?"

Before the surprised doctor could answer, Mrs. Canfield fixed her dark eyes on her granddaughter. "Jane, would you ring for Katie, please? We'll discuss poetry some other time. Right now I should prefer a glass of sherry."

# THREE

As far as general table conversation went that Sunday night I would have done much better to have had my supper upstairs on a tray! I quickly discovered that the doctor and Mrs. Canfield had both traveled abroad, while I had never been out of Massachusetts. They began comparing impressions of places they had been and things they had seen, discussing some doors made by a man named Ghiberti, and something else called the Lion of Lucerne, about neither of which did I know anything. From time to time Dr. Frost would look at me with a politely expectant expression, but since there was no intelligent contribution that I could make, I could do no more than smile at him. As the meal went on, the smile became more fixed. Boredom crept over me, and I began to feel so countrified and lumpish that gradually I drifted into soothing thoughts of Martin. I was quite unprepared when Mrs. Canfield directed a remark to me.

"The Women's Social and Political Union, for example," she said. "What do you think, Louisa, of giving women the right to vote?"

I was too embarrassed to admit that I had not been listening to the talk, nor had I ever thought very much about women's rights. I could feel myself blushing as I tried desperately to reply.

"Why, I . . . I suppose women could vote as well as men," I stammered. "*I* wouldn't know much about voting, but some women are quite intelligent."

"I don't believe women would vote intelligently," Dr. Frost said. "I think they would vote emotionally."

That aroused me! He sounded so patronizing! "Perhaps that might not be altogether bad," I said. "I cannot see that the 'intelligent' voting of men has made the world such a perfect place."

"And you really believe that the unpredictable emotions of females would improve matters?" One of his dark eyebrows lifted maddeningly.

" 'Females,' as you call them, are not always unpredictable, Doctor. For instance, when they are teased they are predictably annoyed!"

"I beg your pardon, Miss Amory! I had no intention of teasing you."

"Then you must consider women quite insensitive."

"In all honesty, Miss Amory, I must admit that I know very little about women except as patients. And as patients they are much easier to deal with than men."

"It's generous of you to say so. But I wasn't speaking of *sick* women. I was speaking of healthy, normal, everyday women!"

"I can see that I have a lot to learn about healthy, normal, everyday women. It will take some intensive study. I don't suppose you'd care to—"

"Offer myself as a textbook? No, thank you, Doctor. I would not make a patient teacher."

"A pity. You would certainly make an attractive one."

I took a deep breath. As Mrs. Canfield's guest I did not want to risk being rude, and yet Dr. Frost's air of amused superiority made me fume. With such dignity as I could muster I turned to Mrs. Canfield.

"It must be past Jane's bedtime," I said. "If you would excuse us—" I rose.

"If you think best, Louisa. But you will join us again, won't you?"

Immediately Dr. Frost was on his feet. "Please do," he urged. "Otherwise I shall feel that you are really annoyed with me."

I wanted to say, "I am!" but I wouldn't give him the satisfaction. "If it is not too late," I murmured. "Come, Jane."

Jane groaned softly, but she knew better than to argue. We left the dining room and went upstairs.

While I hung Jane's dress in her wardrobe she struggled with the buttons on her Ferris waist.

"I don't see why children always have to go to bed," she grumbled. "Just when things start to get interesting, it's always bedtime!"

"*You* may think all that talk about doors and lions and emotional women is interesting. *I* don't!"

"Anyway, Dr. Frost is handsome, isn't he? I think he's a lot handsomer than Martin."

I untied the bows from her hair and separated the braids with my fingers. "You are entitled to your opinion," I said coldly.

Apparently sensing my rough edges, she tried to soothe them. "You looked beautiful in your white dress, Louisa." Then she spoiled it by adding, "Dr. Frost thought so too."

Her hair snapped as I brushed it vigorously. "Don't be silly! He thinks I'm a complete dodo!"

"Maybe he does," she admitted with annoying candor, "but he still thinks you're pretty. He looked at you and I could see him getting all soft around the edges."

"Well, I hope he gets softer and softer until he melts!" I said inanely. "Go and brush your teeth."

A few minutes later I tucked her into the high brass bed and kissed her good night. As I pressed the light switch by the door she said, "Louisa, you know what?"

"What?"

"I bet Emily's plenty mad at Dr. Frost thinking you're pretty! She was going to marry him!"

"Well, it's too bad she didn't grow up and do just that! A bad-tempered, self-centered girl, and a know-it-all, show-offy man! A perfect combination!"

"Louisa?"

"Now what?"

"Please don't talk like that. Don't say things against Emily. It makes her mad. And when Emily was mad, she was *dreadful!*"

I paused for a second, and then went back to the bed and took her hand. "Jane," I said firmly, "stop thinking about Emily Canfield! She was a little girl who died a long time ago. She no longer knows anything, nor feels anything, nor gets 'mad' about anything! She just . . . rests quietly."

Her voice was surprisingly meek. "I hope you're right this time, Louisa. I really, truly do!"


As I came into the parlor Dr. Frost rose and Mrs. Canfield turned to me, smiling.

"I was just telling Adam how much I enjoy

having Jane here this summer," she said. "I did not realize how greatly I missed a child around the place."

"Rather like having Emily back?" the doctor asked, reseating himself near me.

"I suppose, in essence, that's what it is," Mrs. Canfield agreed. "Yet how different the two little girls are!"

"Do you think so? As I remember Emily, Jane looks a great deal like her."

"Yes, there is a strong family resemblance. But I was thinking more of temperament. Jane is a quiet child, thoughtful and obedient. Her father was the same way. But not Emily."

Dr. Frost spoke feelingly. "Emily was a hellion!"

My eyebrows lifted in surprise. This was the first time I had heard Emily spoken of by anyone except her mother, and this new opinion startled me.

Mrs. Canfield sighed. "Well, she was certainly . . . difficult," she said. Then she smiled. "Do you recall how Emily always said she was going to marry you, Adam?"

He laughed. "I do, indeed. I never had anything to say about it. Emily never *asked* me, she simply announced that was what she had planned."

"And you never demurred," Mrs. Canfield added.

"Not for long. It was much easier to go along with Emily than to have my face scratched when I disagreed."

"Yes, that is the way it was. Easier to go along with Emily than to disagree about anything." There was the briefest pause, then Mrs. Canfield smoothly changed the subject. "And now tell me,

Adam. What are your plans? Are you home for good to work with your father?"

The talk continued for another half hour or so. When the little French clock on the mantelpiece chimed ten, Dr. Frost got to his feet.

"I hope we haven't bored you, Miss Amory. You have been very quiet all evening."

I tried to sound polite. "Oh, no," I said brightly. "It has been fascinating."

Looking very small beside the doctor, Mrs. Canfield laid her hand on his arm. "Adam, you must come here often this summer. Louisa needs young company."

I felt like a homely child being pushed forward by its mother! "Oh, I'm sure Dr. Frost is a very busy man—" I began, but he interrupted.

"Not nearly as busy as I hope to be. Thank you for a delicious supper, and for . . ." he paused and glanced at me, "for *stimulating* conversation! This has been a delightful evening."

And with that barbed remark, he left.

Usually when I went to bed I lay and thought about Martin. Remembering his soft voice, his soft blond hair, the strong sweet smell of the pomade he used to keep it smooth, all worked as a sort of lullaby to put me to sleep. But tonight I could not seem to concentrate on him. Instead I kept hearing Dr. Frost's deep voice saying, "Emily was a hellion!" and "It was much easier to go along with Emily than to have my face scratched." I recalled the odd note in Lydia Canfield's voice when she spoke of her daughter as being difficult. There had been no sadness, no regret, such as I felt whenever I thought of Charlotte. What kind of a child could Emily have been? What sort of little girl could die when still so young, and leave this kind of dark memory?

Sometime later I drifted off into a restless sleep, filled with confused dreams of a faceless Emily raising threatening, clawing hands, screaming, "Look out for me, Louisa, I'm a difficult hellion! Look out for me, Louisa—" And suddenly the sound of my name woke me, and it was Jane's voice calling.

"Louisa," I heard again.

I slipped out from under the sheet into the warm summer darkness of my room and went quietly to Jane's door. In a faint glow of light I could see her sitting up in bed.

"What is it, dear?"

"Louisa, what's that light?" she said, and her voice had a hushed sound, almost of fear.

"What light, Jane?"

"There—on my wall. A reflection or something. See it?"

On the wall opposite the garden windows, just above her bed, I could see a soft white blur of light. It was steady, and vaguely round, and very pale. It made Jane's eyes enormous dark pools in her small face.

"Why, it's moonlight, Jane. It must be."

She shook her head. "No, it isn't." Pushing back the cover, she slid out of the bed and went to the garden windows. "Louisa, come here."

I moved to stand beside her. Below us the garden lay in silent blackness, scenting the night. In the very center the reflecting ball stood, and its silver sphere glowed with a pure white light.

"How lovely!" I breathed. "The moonlight shin-

ing on that ball. That's what is reflected here in
your room."

Jane slipped her hand into mine, and hers was
shockingly cold. "Louisa," she whispered. "Look
at the sky."

I raised my eyes to the pitch-dark tent overhead, even as I heard the first gentle pattering of
rain.

"There isn't any moon, Louisa."

Suddenly I felt as chilled as though the night
were midwinter. Outside the window I could hear
the sharp little sound of raindrops on the thick
leaves of the tulip tree. As Jane and I stood there
together we saw the white glow of the reflecting
ball begin to lessen, and in a minute the garden
lay unseen in utter darkness.

"Come to bed, Jane. It's gone now. It was nothing, dear—just some sort of reflection."

She allowed me to lead her toward the bed and
pull the light cover over her.

"Reflection of what, Louisa?" she asked, and
her voice was very small.

"Oh, darling, I don't know. The streetlamp,
most likely."

"But there aren't any streetlamps in the back
of the house."

I felt a strange reluctance to discuss it, that
strange, white, sourceless light. "Jane, I don't
know what it was. But it's gone now, and you must
just go back to sleep. It's very late."

She turned away from me and burrowed into
the pillow, as if for comfort. "All right, Louisa."

The soft obedience in her voice made me want
to comfort her. "It's nothing to worry about, Jane.
Just don't think about it anymore." She didn't

answer, and after a moment I said, "Would you like me to stay with you until you go to sleep?"

She sounded very small, and somehow very alone. "No, thank you. I'm all right now."

"Well, good night then."

"Good night, Louisa."

I went back into my own room, and to bed, but it was not until the rain had stopped and the sky had started to lighten with early dawn that I slept.

# FOUR

I woke the next morning with a heavy, oppressed feeling that I could not at first explain. Then, slowly, things came sifting back. The dinner conversation, Dr. Frost's exasperating superiority, the strange remarks about Emily—the reflecting ball! My eyes flew open. Jane! Was she all right?

Out of bed, I crossed past the windows on my way to her room, and glanced out. The morning was warm and damp after the rain, and Jane was already outdoors, walking delightedly barefoot in the wet grass. Since I had not been up to braid her hair it hung down her back, tied away from her face with a crisp bow. Katie must have done that, I thought. Jane had her jump rope looped over her shoulder, and when she reached the wide clear space, framed by flower beds, at the far end of the garden, she carefully arranged the ends of the rope just so in her hands and then began to jump. I could hear her chanting to herself, and I smiled as I saw her long hair flopping up and down, and the full skirt of her yellow dress bouncing. I could sense how cool and wet the grass must feel beneath her feet. As I watched, I heard Katie's voice calling from the kitchen door below me.

"Jane? Come along now, girl, and have your

breakfast. The cinnamon buns are just hot from the oven."

"I'm coming, Katie."

With one last burst of skipping, just as fast as she could, she took the rope in one hand and started up the lawn toward the back door. Just as she came abreast of the reflecting ball she paused, staring at it. Then, chin high, she marched on by it and I heard the screen door slam lightly as she entered the house. I dressed quickly, a rose-colored cotton skirt and a pale-pink shirtwaist, and—perhaps inspired by Jane—I tied my own hair back with a rose ribbon. Running down the stairs and into the dining room, I found Mrs. Canfield and Jane already at the table. There was a letter from Martin beside my plate, and I slipped it into my lap as I sat down.

"I am so sorry," I said. "I never meant to sleep so late!"

Mrs. Canfield smiled. "My dear, I am delighted that you did. There is no necessity to live by the clock. I only trust it doesn't mean you had a sleepless night."

I glanced quickly at Jane. Her eyes were on her plate as she munched on a large cinnamon bun.

"No, no, not at all. I just . . . well, I just overslept!"

"And a very good morning for it, too. It's going to be dreadfully hot today, I'm afraid. The air seems quite heavy after last night's rain." Mrs. Canfield rang the little silver bell that stood by her place, and after a moment Katie came through the swinging door with a slice of cool, pale-green melon on a chilled plate.

"Morning, Miss Louisa. I'll have your eggs by the time you finish that."

"Good morning, Katie. And thank you for tying Jane's bow. If it *was* you . . ." I looked hesitantly at Mrs. Canfield.

"It's a fine thing to be fixing a little girl's hair again," Katie said. "I haven't your skill with braids, Miss Louisa, but there was many a time I used to tie Miss Emily's hair ribbons."

Placing the melon in front of me, she returned to the kitchen.

"What kind of hair did Emily have?" asked Jane.

"About the color of yours," Mrs. Canfield said. "Perhaps a little darker. It was very curly and I used to brush it around my finger to make ringlets. She wore two little bows to tie it back on each side of her face."

"Was she pretty?"

"I thought so."

"Do you think I'm pretty?"

"Jane!" I exploded. "You know better than to ask a question like that!"

She looked at me, her large eyes calm. "I just wondered," she said. "It's hard to tell about yourself, you know."

Mrs. Canfield looked at Jane with fond amusement. "You need not fret, Jane," she said. "When the time comes that prettiness is most important to you, you will have no cause to worry. Now. Would you like another cinnamon bun?"

"No, thank you. I've had three. May I be excused?"

"Yes, dear. Of course."

Jane disappeared into the kitchen just as Katie set my breakfast plate in front of me. While I ate, Mrs. Canfield poured herself a second cup of coffee.

"Adam was interesting company last night, I thought," she said. "Did you like him, Louisa?"

My eyes were on my plate. "He seemed very nice."

"You were rather quiet all evening. I did hope you were not bored."

"Not at all," I lied smoothly.

She smiled. "Adam has always been quite a talker. Even when he was just a boy, he and Emily would chatter together for hours."

With sudden determination I said, "Mrs. Canfield, have you noticed that Jane seems . . . well, overly preoccupied with . . . with Emily?"

"With Emily?" The older woman looked at me with surprise. "I don't think I know just what you mean."

"I'm not sure I know just what I mean, either. It's only that Jane seems to take every opportunity to speak of Emily, to ask about her. Sometimes she even volunteers statements about her that she seems so . . . so *sure* of!"

"What, for example?"

"Well, she says she feels Emily is around here all the time."

"I think you make too much of such things, Louisa. The young have no conception of death, yet it has a mysterious appeal for them. I think Jane is simply rather intrigued by knowing that another little girl, one to whom she is related, lived here, played here, and—finally—died here."

"Perhaps," I said doubtfully, but after a second's thought I rushed on. "But Jane doesn't even seem to think of Emily as dead. It is more as though she were still here—Emily, I mean. I told you Jane said she could 'feel' her."

"Jane is imaginative, and sensitive, and probably lonely, Aren't imaginary playmates natural under such circumstances?"

"I suppose they are," I said. I was unsatisfied, and yet I could find no words to express the uneasiness I felt. Lydia Canfield was quite right. It was doubtless the result of a very active imagination feeding on a ready-made situation.

Just as we were about to leave the table the doorbell rang, and presently Katie entered the dining room, carrying a florist's box which she gave to Mrs. Canfield.

"A delivery boy just brought it," she said.

Mrs. Canfield lifted the pince-nez that were attached to a little gold clip on the bosom of her dress. Placing them on her nose, she looked at the box carefully.

"Dear me," she murmured. "Whoever do you suppose is sending flowers?"

She untied the single string and raised the lid. Turning back green paper, she lifted a cluster of deep red roses from the box. "How lovely! But from whom? Ah, here is the card." She read it silently, her eyes bright behind the glasses. "Well, I am glad to see that young Adam still remembers his manners. Flowers for his hostess. He writes, 'Thank you so much for a delightful evening! Would you and Jane and Miss Amory be my guests at a Fourth of July band concert in the park tomorrow evening? I shall call for you at eight o'clock. Gratefully, Adam.' Now, isn't that thoughtful of him!"

"Very," I said, unenthusiastically.

"Gracious! I haven't been to a band concert in years! I think we are all going to enjoy ourselves tremendously!"

I wasn't as sure as she was, but I let it go.

Upstairs I made Jane's and my beds and tidied our rooms, deliberately putting off the pleasure of opening Martin's letter. Presently, however, I settled into the little armchair by the window and, slitting the envelope with my finger, drew out the folded pages. The large writing sprawled across them.

"Dear Louisa," I read. "I did not get any letter from you today. In fact I haven't had one for four days. I suppose you are very busy, going to one party after another." I snorted. The nearest thing to a party had been an evening of conversation I couldn't even understand! "I haven't called on any girls since you have been away, mostly because I haven't had much time, working in McHenry's Drug Store as I do. I did walk Susie Pepper home once or twice after she had come in just about closing time for a chocolate soda, but she doesn't really mean anything to me. I would never write poetry to Susie Pepper, even though she is a very nice girl and has invited me to take her to the Milford Fourth of July celebration."

I stopped for a moment and thought about Susie Pepper, a little brown button of a girl with teasing dark eyes that seemed to make boys feel eight feet tall. I had never thought Martin would be interested in anyone like her! So he was taking her to the Fourth of July celebration, was he? Well, I'd write him today and tell him I was going to the Lynn celebration! And I wouldn't set his mind at ease with details or explanations. It might do Martin good to worry a little!

"I think of you a lot, Louisa, and I miss you all the time. I have written a poem to show how well I remember you. Write me soon. Love, Martin."

A poem to show how well he remembered me?

It sounded as though I had been gone for years! I
didn't have any trouble remembering Martin! I
thought about him for a minute, and realized with
a shock that his face was very hazy in my mind!
I knew that he had straight light hair, knew that
his eyes were very large and pale blue and that he
had to wear glasses when he studied. I knew that
his kisses were very sweet—but I couldn't *see*
him! Instead, a totally different face kept flashing
through my mind. Deep, probing eyes under dark
brows that matched the dark, crisp hair, a firm
mouth above a lean, cleft chin—in exasperation
I turned to the last page of Martin's letter to find
the poem. It was titled "An Ode to Louisa's Lovely
Face," and read:

> *Louisa has such yellow hair,*
> *Louisa's lips are red and fair.*
> *Louisa's eyes, now blue, now green—*
> *The loveliest face I've ever seen.*

With unaccountable vexation I decided the four
lines made me sound like a piece of Scotch plaid!
Had Martin's poetry always been as silly as that?
I didn't think it could have been, else how had I
always been so moved and touched by it? In quite
a bad mood I stuffed the pages back into the envelope, added it to the pile in my dresser drawer,
and picking up my writing box, I went downstairs
and out the French doors to the garden.

Jane was sitting curled up in one of the deep,
cushioned wicker chairs under the tulip tree, and
I settled comfortably in the chair next to hers,
grateful for the shade. She had a tablet of paper
on her lap, and she was chewing thoughtfully on
the end of a pencil.

"Thinking great thoughts?" I asked.

"I'm writing a poem."

"I thought you didn't approve of poetry."

She looked at me reproachfully. "I like *good* poetry. I just don't like soppy poems like Martin writes."

"Louisa has such yellow hair, Louisa's lips are red and fair," I thought to myself. Yes, in all honesty it might be called soppy. "I didn't know you were a poet," I said to her.

"I never was before. I just thought I'd try."

"Well, if I can help you, let me know."

I was not too optimistic about the probable result of Jane's efforts. She was never overly inclined toward the written word. She loved to read, and read well, but writing was a chore for her, and her handwriting was still very youthful and unformed.

Feeling as uninspired as Jane looked, I tried to start a letter to Martin. I felt curiously unwilling to tell him how quiet and uneventful my life was in Lynn. If he chose to believe I spun on a carrousel of gaiety, let him! In this mood I wrote of "the fascinating, traveled young doctor" who had dined with us, and who was taking me (I somehow neglected to mention Jane and her grandmother) to the Fourth of July celebration. I wrote that I hoped he would have a pleasant evening with Susie Pepper and that her "constant chatter might not prove too bothersome." I thanked him for his poem and told him that Jane was "trying her hand at amusing little verses, too." And then I signed it "Your friend, Louisa," and shoved it into an envelope. Suddenly feeling quite cheerful, I looked at Jane who had been setting down a few words from time to time, then scratching them out and gazing off into space.

"You look as though it wasn't so easy to be a poet," I said.

"Things just don't come out right."

"I can sympathize. I have the same trouble writing letters. Why don't you leave it for a few minutes and do something else? It just might come easier when you try again."

She looked at me seriously. "Do you really think so?"

"It's possible."

"Well, it's not coming now, so I might as well." She slid out of the chair and, half skipping, went off down the garden. I watched her stop by one of the pansy beds and kneel on the grass, looking closely at the gay flowers.

She stayed quiet for a few minutes, and then she wandered aimlessly in the direction of the reflecting ball. When she was within a few feet of it she paused, and I thought at first she was going to avoid it. Then, as though on second thought, she walked very slowly close to it, placed her hands on either side of it, and—standing on tiptoe —peered in. I wondered with amusement whether she was making faces at herself again, but her back was toward me and I could not see her face.

Suddenly she turned and came running across the grass. Snatching up her pencil and tablet, she threw herself into the chair, pulled her feet under her, and scribbled furiously for a moment.

"There!" she said with triumph. "There's my poem. Do you want to read it?"

"Of course."

She handed me the tablet. In her loosely formed, downhill script I read:

*Robed in velvet, jewel-toned,*
*They stand in small majestic grace.*
*Watching their garden kingdom grow*
*With royal pleasure on each face.*

My delight was sincere, and quite apparent, I'm sure. "Why, Jane! That's charming! It's the pansies, isn't it?"

"Yes. Do you really like it?"

"I'm amazed! I think it's lovely!"

She preened herself with a little wiggle of her shoulders. "You don't need to sound so surprised. I *told* you I was going to be a poet."

A dark suspicion crossed my mind. "Jane. You didn't *read* this anywhere, did you?"

She looked at me indignantly. "No! I just wrote it! Just this minute, while I was sitting here. I walked around, like you said, and I looked at the pansies, and then I came back, but I still hadn't thought of anything to write, and then I looked in the reflecting ball because I didn't want to always be sort of . . . you know, scared of it—after last night—and while I was looking in it all of a sudden I just—" She stopped abruptly, her eyes moving from me to the silver globe.

"What, Jane?" I asked softly. "All of a sudden you just—what?"

Her voice was almost inaudible. "Just knew the whole poem. All of a sudden I just knew it."

A dozen half-formed thoughts flew through my mind, followed immediately by the knowledge that they could not be true.

"You see," I said gently. "I told you it would come if you just stopped trying for a minute."

She got out of the chair and stood close to me. "You really think that was it, Louisa?"

"Why, of course. It almost always works. And it's a very good thing to remember."

"I guess that's what it was, all right," she said doubtfully. Then, with more confidence, she repeated, "Yes, that's what it must have been. I just left it alone for a while and then it—just came to me!"

"Your grandmother will be very proud of you."

"Shall I take it in and show it to her?"

"Why don't you? But don't interrupt her if she's busy with something."

"I won't." Taking the tablet from me, she read again the four lines written there. "It really is very good, isn't it?" she said smugly.

Not a great deal later I was going through the upstairs hall on my way to my room to get a stamp for Martin's letter. As I passed the open door of Mrs. Canfield's room I heard her call me.

"Louisa. Would you come here a moment, please?"

I entered. The room was large and cool, the shades drawn halfway down to keep out most of the sunlight. The furniture was massive and dark, and it seemed an almost overpowering chamber for the very small woman who sat in a straight armchair by the window. Her hands were on the carved arms of the chair, but instead of resting easily as they generally did, the fingers were clenched tightly against the wood.

"Yes, Mrs. Canfield. Can I do something for you?"

"Louisa, sit down a moment." She indicated a small chair by the desk. Puzzled by something in her voice, I sat down quietly.

"Jane brought me a poem a little while ago. She said she had written it."

"Yes. I saw it. I thought it was quite good for a nine-year-old."

"Louisa, did Jane really tell you she had written it herself?"

"Why, I saw her, Mrs. Canfield! She tried for quite a long time, writing a line or two and then crossing it out, and she was becoming very impatient with herself. I suggested she leave it for a few minutes and perhaps it would come easier when she tried again, so she played around the garden for a little while, and then she came back and just sat down and wrote the four lines very quickly."

"I see." There was silence for a moment, then she said, "Open the second drawer of that desk, Louisa. It is not locked. I unlocked it myself just a few minutes ago."

I did as I was told, disclosing a tidy collection of letters, leather-covered books that looked like diaries, photograph albums—all the bits and pieces that strengthen memories.

"On the right there is a purple leather notebook. You see it?"

"Yes." I lifted it, smooth and cool, from the drawer.

"Open it from the back. You find where the writing ends? Several pages from the back?"

"Yes, ma'am."

"Turn back three pages—or is it four? You see a page with a verse on it? At the top is written the title, 'Pansy Song.'"

Even as I said the words, "Yes, I see it here," my eyes were racing down the page, through the four neat lines of exquisite penmanship. At the bottom was written, with something of a flourish, "By Emily Canfield." Slowly I lifted my eyes to the

woman sitting quietly by the window. Leaning
forward, she held out to me the sheet of paper
with Jane's poem on it.

"Compare them," she said.

But I didn't need to. Line for line, word for
word, the verse that Jane had written that morning
and the verse that Emily had written more than a
dozen years ago were absolutely identical.

# FIVE

These "Emily-incidents" bothered me. The fact
that Jane had seen herself in the reflecting ball as
Emily was really no stranger than that she should
have imagined herself to look like Queen Victoria,
or a frog. But her distress when she disclaimed
ever having seen a picture of Emily had been so
real! Was it possible that in this house of well-
preserved memories she had never glimpsed a
photograph of her young aunt? Possible, I supposed, but unlikely. She must have seen one sometime, and simply forgotten.

But what about the light from the reflecting
ball? *Emily's* reflecting ball? There had not been
a moon. There were no streetlights in the rear of
the house, as Jane had pointed out. Everyone had
been in bed and there were no lights burning in
any of the rooms. Yet how could I be sure of that?
Mrs. Canfield—even Katie—might have left one
on downstairs, either intentionally or inadver-
tently. If that were the case there was no mystery
whatever.

As for Jane's poem, someone—sometime—
might have read it to her. With her deep interest
in the pansies it could well have recurred in her
memory, even though she had no recollection of
having heard it before. So all these things could

be easily explained, if one thought about them logically.

And yet, for reasons I could not understand, these rational explanations did not satisfy me at all!

Fourth of July was hot and sunny, but there was a pleasant dry breeze. I washed Jane's hair and my own in the morning, and then we sat outdoors in the sun to dry it. I pulled a comb gently and easily through Jane's long straight silky mane. In my own hair the comb caught and pulled and knotted in the curls until I despaired of ever getting the snarls out.

"I don't see why I have to have a headful of lamb's wool," I said crossly. "Why couldn't I have nice smooth shining hair like yours, Jane?"

"If you did, you'd wish it was curly."

"Oh, no, I wouldn't!"

"Yes, you would. I wish *mine* was. Couldn't I put curling rags in mine, Louisa?"

"And have it come out looking like corkscrews? No! Just be grateful your hair is the way it is!"

"Emily had corkscrew curls. Grandmother said so."

I tugged viciously at the comb as it hit a particularly stubborn place. "Emily again! I don't care whether Emily's hair was bright green and grew in little bowknots all over her head! You are you and Emily was Emily and you are two different people and don't ever forget it! Besides, I'm tired of hearing about her!"

Jane grinned at me. "My, you are in a state today. Is it because we're going to see Dr. Frost tonight?"

"Certainly not!"

"I like him, Louisa. Do you?"

"I neither like him nor dislike him. I just don't think about him."

"Do you think about Martin?"

"Oh, Jane," I said in exasperation. "Can't you talk about anything except Martin or Dr. Frost? Martin's a very nice boy but I haven't seen him in weeks, and the doctor's a bore who talks about things I never heard of, and I don't care if I never see him again! There must be something else you can talk about!"

"I could talk about Emily," she offered.

"And Emily's *dead!* So just forget her, too! Now, turn around so I can braid your hair."

Jane gave me a long troubled look before she swiveled around on the grass. "I'd *like* to forget Emily, Louisa. I really would. She just won't let me."

I opened my mouth for a sharp retort, but something in her voice stopped me. Instead I leaned forward and kissed her sun-warmed hair before I started to plait it.

The prospect of seeing Dr. Frost again might not excite me, but the thought of a band concert and fireworks did. As I put on a blue skirt and my newest white shirtwaist, the one with the lace jabot, I thought hopefully that with music going on, there wouldn't be much opportunity for conversation, which would be all to the good. I clipped red bows to my white slippers, tied one in my hair, and was ready at eight o'clock when a great roaring and chuffing sounded outside the house.

Jane peered out of the parlor window to see Dr.

Frost stepping down from a shining automobile. When the doorbell rang she could not wait for Katie, but went rushing to answer it herself.

"Is it yours? Are we going to ride in it? Will you blow the horn? A *lot*?"

"Yes, yes, yes, and yes." Dr. Frost came into the parlor, Jane's hand in his. "Good evening, Mrs. Canfield. Miss Amory. I suggest light scarves for your hair. It is apt to get a little windy."

"Good gracious," Lydia Canfield murmured, gazing out of the window at the gleaming motor. "I have only ridden in an automobile two or three times before. I'm not at all sure—"

"I am," Dr. Frost said firmly. "You will enjoy it! It is quite safe, and very comfortable."

He helped us into the car, Jane and I in the back, and Mrs. Canfield sitting beside him.

"But you should be sitting with Louisa. I shall be quite all right in back with Jane."

The doctor patted her hand. "On the way home, perhaps. In case you get panicky and start to jump I want to be where I can grab you."

"Jump, Adam! Mercy! I won't dare to stir!"

He laughed, gave the crank a few strong turns, and we swung out of the drive and onto the street, becoming one of many automobiles all going in the direction of the park. Beside me Jane was in absolute bliss, holding her red-and-white-checked gingham dress down across her knees, feeling the wind in her face. In the front seat Mrs. Canfield sat erect, her feet planted firmly on the floor, her hands folded tightly in her lap. Dr. Frost drove easily and well, and it wasn't more than a few moments before Lydia Canfield began to relax a little. She turned her head from side to side, noticing the other motor cars, showing interest in the people strolling along the sidewalks. Presently she turned part way round in the seat.

"This is really very pleasant, isn't it, Louisa?" she shouted. I smiled and nodded, and she turned back, sitting more easily now, enjoying herself just as Dr. Frost had promised she would.

The park was beginning to fill as Dr. Frost helped us all from the car. From a trunk on the back of the automobile he took a red plaid wool rug and two small folding stools, then extended his other arm to Mrs. Canfield. Jane and I followed, and we walked across the grass to a spot where we could see the bandstand clearly.

Mrs. Canfield and I sat comfortably on the little canvas stools, while Jane and Dr. Frost settled on the rug at our feet. The band was just tuning up, and Jane giggled at the odd honks, snorts, and toots of the various instruments. Dr. Frost brought out his pipe and filled it, and then sat, knees drawn up and arms loosely around them, puffing contentedly. The Band Master tapped his baton against his music rack, there was a moment of silence, and then the marvelous, exciting blast of a Sousa march filled the park.

Jane said, "Ah!" in satisfaction, Mrs. Canfield's slippered toe tapped ever so slightly in time to the music, and Dr. Frost whistled the melody softly between his teeth. As for me, I shivered with delight as the waves of music washed around us.

There were the occasional pop-pop-pops of small firecrackers lighted by little boys on the fringes of the crowd. There was a smell of punk, its pungent scent helping to ward off mosquitoes. As the night grew darker there were the enchanted golden explosions of sparklers and, from somewhere a little distance away, the multicolored parabola of a skyrocket. The bandstand gleamed under the bright electric lights, the brass instruments looked bold and shining, the navy blue and red and gold uniforms of the musicians seemed splendid indeed. I was sorry when it was all over.

We walked slowly back to the automobile, but this time Mrs. Canfield took Jane's hand firmly in hers and they went on ahead. Dr. Frost offered me his arm, and I had no choice but to take it. People passed us on both sides of the hard dirt path, and he allowed them to come between us and the other two.

After a few idle comments on the concert he said, "Louisa Amory, will you have dinner with me sometime this week?"

Surprised by the sudden invitation, I didn't know what to say. "Well, I'm not sure . . . there's Jane, you see—"

"Jane is not included," he said flatly. "Do you like lobster?"

"Oh, I adore lobster! But—"

"Friday? I'll pick you up at six."

His confidence irked me. "I will speak to Mrs. Canfield. If she doesn't mind—"

"She won't mind. Friday, then."

"I'll look forward to it," I said weakly. "Thank you."

When we reached home we all stood for a moment at the door. The night stretched above us, dark and star-pinned, lit from time to time with the beautiful flashes of fireworks.

"I cannot thank you enough, Adam," Mrs. Canfield said. "I don't know when I have enjoyed an evening more!"

"On the strength of that, may I induce you to part with Louisa on Friday? I should like to take her out to dinner."

There was no hesitation in her reply, and I suddenly wondered if the whole idea might have been hers. "Splendid! I have felt quite guilty about her staying at home every night. She should certainly get out more!"

Jane's dark eyes had been going from one to the other of us, and now she started silently hopping up and down, singing to herself in an almost inaudible voice. "I bet it's going to happen! I bet it's going to happen!"

I hoped Dr. Frost wouldn't hear her, but it was an idle hope.

"And just exactly what is it that you bet is going to happen, Jane?" he asked.

I pinioned Jane with the most threatening glare I could manage, and her eyes dropped demurely.

"Oh, I don't think you'd be interested, Dr. Frost," she said. "At least, not quite *yet!*"

# SIX

The next morning I woke to a dark, humid, threatening day, and by the time we had finished breakfast thunder was rolling distantly and the first heavy sluggish raindrops were falling.

About midmorning Mrs. Canfield came into the laundry room in the basement where I was pressing out Jane's and my ribbons while Katie did the larger ironing. The little pot stove heated our irons, and the basement, smelling pleasantly of soap and starch and fresh clothes, was dry and warm.

"Jane is moping about, completely desolate," Mrs. Canfield said. "I thought perhaps this might be a good time to make a visit to the attic and see whether we can unearth any playthings for her."

"Of course! It's a wonderful idea! And just the day for it. I'll put these ribbons away and join you."

Jane was excited by the suggestion. "Oh, yes! What a good thing to do!" She was out of the bedroom door and into the hallway, calling, "Grandmother? Where are you? Louisa says we're going up to the attic!"

Lydia Canfield led the way along the carpeted corridor to the staircase that rose from the far end. "I don't recall what may be up there," she said. "It must be years since I've even been in the place."

At the top of the angular stairs there was a large hall. The first door stood open, and I could see Katie's immaculate room, looking lived in and comfortable.

Next came a bathroom, the tub setting high on white claw feet, and after that another small bedroom, apparently unused. Opposite these was a closed door. Mrs. Canfield turned the white china knob, but I had to help her push against the door to open it.

The moment it was opened we could hear the rain beating heavily on the raftered roof. The air in the room was unmoving, filled with the scent of mustiness, of old books and papers, of leather trunks and valises, of mothballs and camphor and dust. So little light came in through the two tiny windows tucked under the eaves that we could barely see. Mrs. Canfield pushed the electric switch by the door, and a small bulb cast a dim light through the center of the room. The shadows in the corners hung deep. Jane inhaled with pleasure.

"It's nice!" she said. "All cobwebby and moldy! Oh, *look* at all the things!"

Around three sides of the large room ranged trunks and barrels and boxes, and on a rod along the fourth side hung suits and dresses. An umbrella stand held canes, parasols, two or three ancient rifles and a rusting sword. A small sidesaddle rested on a wooden sawhorse, and I could see a doll carriage made of wicker with a sunshade dangling over it, a large and lavish dollhouse, boxes of games and piles of books.

Jane gave a little hop of excitement. "Oh, Grandmother! May I *poke*?"

Mrs. Canfield laughed. It was a particularly pretty laugh, and I thought in amazement that it was the first time I had heard it.

"Yes, child. Go ahead and poke. I'm sure everything is covered with dust, but I don't suppose you care."

While Jane clambered around trunks and barrels, peering into boxes, I wandered along the rack of clothes. A number of dresses hung close together, looking like a rainbow. Shining satin, crisp taffeta, and soft velvet, sheer summer cottons, some very elegant and formal, others quite simple.

"These are beautiful, Mrs. Canfield," I said. "Whose were they?"

She came to stand beside me. "Those? They were mine."

"What lovely colors!" I found it difficult to imagine Lydia Canfield wearing anything but her constant black.

"Yes, they are, aren't they?" She smoothed the soft pile of a glowing garnet velvet gown. "Mr. Canfield and I went to New York one winter—just for a week. I wore this to a first night performance at Daly's Theatre."

"How long ago was that?" I asked.

"Oh, I can't think precisely. Emily was about four then—four or five—that must make it close to twenty years ago. We left Emily and John with Katie and the nursemaid, a nice young woman. Her name was Miss Simmons. Oh dear, what a fearsome time they had with Emily!"

"In what way?"

"She refused to eat, she simply stormed and cried and shrieked herself into a high fever." Mrs.

Canfield gazed thoughtfully at the rich deep red. "I had forgotten that week."

"But why? What upset her so?"

"She did not want her father and me to leave her."

"But surely she was well cared for, and with her brother here——"

Mrs. Canfield turned her eyes to me, and they were quiet and brooding. "You did not know Emily, Louisa."

I could not imagine why the sturdy Katie had not administered a firm hand in punishment for such behavior. Surely, whatever Miss Simmons may have been, Katie was not one to tolerate temper tantrums. "I don't suppose Emily won out in this case, though, did she?" I asked.

"As a matter of fact, she did. Poor Miss Simmons was so distraught after a few days of this that she sent Mr. Canfield a telegram. He insisted we come home immediately. I remember how disappointed I was. We had planned to stay longer."

"It hardly seems possible," I began, and then stopped, realizing that any sort of judgment from me would be impertinent.

"It hardly seems possible that a child should not be better controlled. Is that what you were thinking? Or that she should have been so indulged? I can understand—but that is the way things were."

From a far corner of the attic came Jane's somewhat muffled voice. "I found a wonderful trunkful of things! Oh, I wish there was more light!"

I hardly heard Jane. My mind was still on Emily. It seemed incomprehensible to me that

Mrs. Canfield should have permitted such behavior in her child.

Almost as though she read my thoughts Lydia Canfield said, "Looking back, I can see where I should have resisted more often, been firmer, for Emily's own sake. But it would have distressed her father, and . . . I loved him very much. It would have been most difficult to disregard his wishes."

"But could Mr. Canfield not see that such indulgence was harmful?"

"No, I think he could not. Emily was so charming—so irresistible—when things went as she wished. Often there were two or three weeks at a stretch when no one could have been more delightful than our daughter. Those were the times when my husband would point out to me that 'giving in to her,' as he said I called it, seemed not to be spoiling her at all. He wanted so much for her to be always happy! He . . . he *adored* her, Louisa. There is no other word for it."

I began to understand better, then. I could see that while Mrs. Canfield might well have had the strength of character to forbid or deny Emily certain requests, it would have been nearly impossible for her to override her husband, possibly even to anger him with her discipline. But surely John could not have been treated in the same permissive manner. I asked about him.

"No, John was raised quite differently, but then John was quite a different sort of child. I could reason with him, which I never could with Emily, and he would accept explanations. John and I were very close, always. Then, too, his father felt that a strict upbringing was quite proper for a boy. It was only Emily, you see. From the moment she was born she was the center of my husband's life. There was nothing he would not do for her."

I had almost forgotten Jane in thinking about that faraway child, Emily, when I heard the small voice again from the corner, annoyed.

"If somebody would just *help* me a little bit instead of standing and talking, I could get this trunk out where I could see it!"

I laughed and went to her, wending my way through the clutter in the dusky attic.

"I'm sorry, dear. What are you trying to do?"

"I *told* you! I'm trying to drag this trunk out where there's more light!"

I took hold of one leather strap on the side of the large old metal trunk and pulled it across the floor, Jane pushing sturdily from the back.

I opened the curved lid. In the top tray lay a number of dolls, their pretty faces smiling vacantly, except for one whose wax features were hideously misshapen.

"Oh, what a shame," I said. "Look. Her face has melted. I expect this attic gets very hot during the summer."

"No—no, it wasn't the attic heat. Emily—" Mrs. Canfield stopped.

Jane's eyes widened in horror. "You mean Emily did that? On *purpose*?"

There was no answer. The attic was very still for a moment. Then Jane shivered.

"I don't like to look at it," she said. "Cover it up, Louisa."

Silently Mrs. Canfield handed me a pale-pink shawl which she took from the clothes rack, and I gently wrapped the disfigured plaything in it and laid it to one side. Jane watched me, her eyes somber.

But there were other things in the lower part of
the trunk that quickly took her mind away from
the doll. Sets of blocks, a game of dominoes, delicate wooden jackstraws with their tiny hook. A
wooden box with a sliding lid held a schoolroom
with pupils and desks and the schoolmaster, each
a flat wooden piece, brightly painted, and each
with its small grooved base to hold it upright. As
Jane discovered each new treasure I rose, dusted
off my skirt, and wandered about the room. In
one corner stood a chipped white-painted wooden
pedestal, topped with a saucer-shaped piece.

"What stood on this?" I asked idly. "It seems to
have been meant to hold something particular."

Mrs. Canfield joined me. "Oh, yes. Yes, that
used to hold a reflecting ball in the garden. Like
the one we have now."

"What happened to it?"

"It was broken."

There was an odd inflection in her voice that
prevented me from asking any more. "Oh," was all
I said. After a moment, gazing at the empty pedestal, Lydia Canfield went on, a strange smile on her
face.

"Emily was always enraptured by the silver
ball. She used to stand gazing into it for quite long
periods. One day—she was about ten, I believe—
she had tried her hair a new way which I thought
unbecoming, and I told her so. She was quite
piqued with me, and ran out into the garden. I
stood at the window watching her. I saw her go to
the reflecting ball and stand there, staring into it.
After a moment she stepped back, and, raising her
hands, pushed the ball off the pedestal and onto
the stone that surrounded it. It smashed, of course,
into a thousand pieces. Emily came running into

the house and up to her room, locking herself in. She would not open the door for me all day. When her father came home he went upstairs and she let him in at once. He asked her about the ball— I had told him of the incident—and she said that when she looked into it she saw a face that wasn't hers. It was an ugly face, she said, and she insisted that it must have been the face of someone else who had looked into the ball."

"Of someone else? But surely it was just the distortion such round objects give!"

"Of course it was. Her father tried to explain that to her, but Emily would have no part of it. Other people had been looking into her reflecting ball and she could see their ugly faces. She wanted a new ball, of course, one that only she would be permitted to look into."

"And her father got it for her."

"Naturally. And assured her that no one except Emily would ever look into it. That it was all hers. That is the one that stands out there now."

The rain drummed loud on the attic roof and I could barely hear Jane's voice above it. She sat cross-legged on the floor, cradling one of the dolls in her arms. She did not look up as she spoke.

"*I* looked into Emily's silver ball," she said. "I didn't know I wasn't supposed to."

"But of course you can, Jane," Mrs. Canfield answered. "It isn't Emily's any longer, you know."

Jane raised her eyes slowly to her grandmother's face. "Yes, it is," she said. "Emily's face still lives in it. I have seen it there."

"Nonsense, dear. You have seen the distortions, that's all. Just as Louisa said. Because the glass is curved—"

Jane interrupted. "No, Grandmother. It wasn't

dis——, what you said. It was Emily in there. She looked out at me. I saw her."

Mrs. Canfield's eyes met mine for a long moment. Then she forced a smile. "I think we had better go downstairs now," she said. "This old attic is making us all quite fanciful!"

It was with relief that I closed the door behind us.

# SEVEN

On Friday morning my daily letter from Martin arrived and I put it in my pocket to read later. I was busy with several small chores—some mending for Mrs. Canfield, helping Jane set up in her room the dollhouse which Jacob had brought down from the attic, pressing my yellow voile dress to wear that evening—so it wasn't until afternoon that I put my hand in my pocket for my handkerchief and felt the letter there. A little ashamed of my forgetfulness, I wandered out into the garden to read it.

The summer afternoon was hushed, with the shade stretching across the grass as the sun drooped lower. Fat bumblebees droned over the roses, a few butterflies made their staccato way from zinnia to balsam to phlox, resting still-winged for a second, and then zigzagging off again. I sat in my favorite chair under the tulip tree and pulled Martin's letter from its envelope.

"Dear Louisa," it said. "This will have to be a pretty short letter because I am going to Susie Pepper's house for supper. She's really a very nice girl and she thinks it's wonderful that I can write poetry. I showed her some I had written, but not any about you. She says she wishes I'd write some

to her, but I haven't. I don't know why you thought
Susie's talking might bother me. It doesn't at all.
She asked me if I had heard from you and I told
her about your letter—the one that said you were
going to the Fourth of July celebration with that
doctor. Susie says if he is a doctor he must be
pretty old, and to tell you she's sorry you have to
go out with old men. She sends you her love. So do
I. Martin."

Impatiently I shoved the letter into the envelope,
not even bothering to fold the pages neatly. Why,
*Jane* could have written a more interesting letter
than that! Feeling quite out of temper, I started
back toward the house. As I crossed the soft lawn
I came to the reflecting ball poised on its standard.
Flagstones set around the base of the pedestal
made a little island in the grass, and I walked
close, stepping onto the stones. Slowly, very slowly,
I leaned to peer into the ball. Its convex surface
made my nose seem large, with the rest of my
face fading back from it, but it was undeniably my
face. That pile of ash-blond hair and those thick-
lashed blue eyes were certainly Louisa Amory's.
There was no trace of Emily in that reflected
picture. It startled me suddenly to realize that I
had not been sure I would see my own face. This
odd business with a dead child is becoming real
to you, I thought. Forget her!

But tell myself what I would, it was as if that
man-made, silvered glass globe, resting on its
painted wooden support, had some power—some
fascination—some life of its own. It was all I
could do to turn away from it and walk quickly
into the house through the kitchen.

Katie was rinsing dishcloths at the sink. "I was

watching you out the window," she said. "I was just coming to tell you it was time you started dressing for that dinner party."

"Not a party, Katie. Just dinner—with Dr. Frost."

She smiled at me. "And isn't that enough party for you?"

I must have looked embarrassed, because she went right on. "He's a fine man, that one. You could do a lot worse, Miss Louisa."

"I'm just having *dinner* with him, Katie. That's all."

"Well, everything has to start somewhere," she observed cheerfully. Then her tone changed. "I saw you out there by that reflecting ball. I keep away from that thing. I want no part of it."

"Oh, Katie, don't! You're beginning to sound as full of weird ideas as Jane!"

"Weird? Maybe so. But you didn't know Emily."

"That's what everyone keeps telling me," I said sharply, "and it's quite true. I didn't. But the child has been dead for a dozen years or more, and as sorry as I am that she died so young, nothing she used to do can make any difference to anyone or anything now!"

"It's making a difference to Jane. You know that yourself, Miss Louisa." She paused, and then went on. "That doll she found in the attic—the one with the melted face. She asked me how it happened."

"Did you tell her, Katie? Did you know?"

"Yes, I knew. But I didn't tell her. I think she knew most of it herself, somehow."

"What did happen to the doll?"

"Emily lost her temper with it one day because it wouldn't stand up. She held its face over my stove. Held it there until it melted. She said that would be a lesson to it."

I could feel my lips tighten with distaste. "How —how awful! But Katie, why do you think Jane knows?"

"When she asked me I told her I couldn't remember. But she stood there—looking at the stove. Then she said, 'That doll's face was made of wax. Wax melts easily, doesn't it, Katie?' I told her yes. And she kept staring at the stove, and all she said was, 'Oh, Emily! *Why?*'"

"I see," I said. Somehow the cheerful kitchen did not seem so cheerful. "Well, whatever she may have been, Emily is dead now. Let the poor girl rest in peace."

"I'd like nothing better, Miss Louisa! Nothing better in the whole world!"

There seemed nothing more to say. I went up the back stairs and as I entered my room Jane looked up from the dollhouse.

"Are you going to dress now, Louisa?"

"Yes," I said abstractedly.

"May I sit on your bed and watch?"

"I suppose so, if you really want to. It's hardly all that exciting, though."

"It is to me." She came bouncing through the doorway and threw herself down on my bed. "Are you going to wear the white dress again?"

"No. The yellow one."

"Oh. That's too bad. He would probably propose to you if you wore the white one."

"You know, Jane," I said rather huffily, "you really must learn not to meddle in grown-up affairs!"

Jane sighed. "In a minute you'll tell me to run along and play and let you dress in peace!"

Her tone mimicked mine so well I couldn't help but laugh. "All right," I said. "You win. I'll stop talking like an aunt, and you stop talking like Little Miss Know-it-all."

With good humor restored, Jane lay comfortably on the bed, her chin in her hands, her legs flopping up and down, making occasional comments as she watched me dress. I was just pinning my little cameo brooch into place when we heard the doorbell.

"There he is," Jane said quickly. "I'm going to answer."

Sliding off the bed, she went racing through the hall and down the stairs. Taking a thin scarf from my drawer, and tipping a drop of cologne on my handkerchief before placing it in my drawstring bag, I went along to Mrs. Canfield's room to tell her I was leaving.

"I'm so glad Adam asked you," she said. "Enjoy yourself, Louisa."

"Thank you. I'm sure I will."

Going down the sharply turning staircase, my first glimpse of that dark head, those deep blue eyes looking up at me, made me suddenly almost breathless. Whatever else Dr. Frost might or might not be, he was certainly attractive!

"You know what your aunt looks like, Jane?" he asked.

"What?"

"Like summer. Just like summer coming down the stairs. Good evening, Louisa."

"Good evening—Adam." If he could use first names, then so could I.

"Shall we be on our way?" His eyes were smiling at me, and I began to think the pompous doctor might just possibly be human.

"I'm quite ready." I turned to Jane. "Good night, dear. Go to bed promptly."

Jane pulled me down for a kiss. "He's really very nice, Louisa," she whispered. "Don't be mean to him."

"I'll try not to," I whispered back, and a minute later Adam Frost was helping me into his automobile.

On the drive to the restaurant I found myself telling him about my family, and the house in Milford, and he said he had always liked the town, and perhaps I would allow him to visit there sometime. I said I would, and asked him about his medical career and how he had managed to complete his training so quickly.

"It was quite simple. I managed two years in one."

"Mrs. Canfield told me you were extremely brilliant."

"Not really. It's just that I always knew I would be a doctor. My mother died when I was small, and consequently I spent most of my time with my father. From the time I was eight or nine I used to go on some of his housecalls with him, and a couple of years later I used to help him prepare medications, and lend a hand in setting broken bones or applying dressings. During high school I transcribed some of his notes for him, and I think I read every medical book he owned. By the time I got to studying medicine formally I was pretty far ahead of the other men in the class."

"Are you a *good* doctor?" I asked, smiling at him.

He glanced at me, his eyes teasing. "I think so. Develop a slight sniffle or a minor cough and I'll come and tend you. Then you can see for yourself."

"Thank you," I laughed, "but I'll take your word for your medical talents." I settled back, feeling more comfortable with him than I ever expected to.

The restaurant was on the tip of the little peninsula just below Lynn, and from our table we could look through large open windows at the quiet water of the bay. We had lobster Thermidor, and a fresh, crisp bread, and a salad, with delicious hot coffee.

"Dining out is always exciting to me," I confessed. "It seems so—special!"

"This *is* special," he said. "Do you know this is the first time I've been out with a young lady in— well, months?"

Our eyes met and held. Then I looked away.

"Tell me about Emily," I said abruptly. "Tell me everything you remember about her."

He looked surprised. "How did we suddenly get to Emily?"

"It isn't sudden. Please. Tell me what you can."

He took a sip of coffee, set the cup down gently, and sat in silence for a minute. "Emily was the most strong-willed person I ever knew," he said presently. "I can't think of a time in her short life when she didn't get whatever she had set her heart on. It never mattered to her whether something was right or wrong, or whether it might hurt someone else. If it pleased Emily—that was all that mattered."

"Mrs. Canfield told me that Emily's father could deny her nothing. She said that he adored his daughter."

"I expect he did. The Canfield family hadn't pro-

"She wanted her own way. She begged and cajoled her mother, and Mrs. Canfield pointed out to her that there were many people who were really very ill and needed the doctor, whereas Emily did not. That the doctor only had time to visit patients who were actually quite sick, and truly needed him. Then Emily asked her mother if Dr. Frost would come if she got very sick indeed, and Mrs. Canfield assured her that he would. Of course he would. And that was all it took."

"But I still don't understand."

"Mrs. Canfield offered to stay and read to Emily, but Emily said—ever so sweetly—that she thought she would have a little nap as soon as she finished her lunch, so her mother left her. At Emily's request Mrs. Canfield closed the door, telling her to call when she woke up. Emily never called. Mrs. Canfield, probably glad of the peace, didn't go back for two or three hours."

"And then?" I found I was sitting forward, my hands folded tight on the edge of the table.

"As she went along the upstairs corridor she could feel cold air from somewhere. When she opened Emily's door the room was freezing."

"And Emily?"

"Emily had apparently emptied the water from her bedside carafe over her nightgown. She had pulled an armchair in front of the window, opened it wide, and was sitting there—drenched to the skin, and quite blue with cold. By that time her chest was so congested she could barely breathe. She was nearly unconscious."

I stared at him in amazement. "You mean she was deliberately trying to make herself very ill?"

"I told you Emily had ways of getting what she wanted," Adam said quietly.

"And she died?"

"Very early the next morning. My father came, without me, ironically, but he could do nothing for her."

I shivered, and Adam reached out and laid one warm hand over mine. "Why do you want to know all this, Louisa? It was a long time ago. It's all over now."

"I'm not sure it is," I said very softly.

His hand tightened. "What do you mean?"

"Oh, Adam, I don't know!" I burst out. "But there have been things since Jane and I have been there—"

"What sort of things?"

"Oh, they sound ridiculous put into words—"

"Try."

"Well, one night—the same night you were there at the house for the first time—there was a strange light in Jane's room. She sleeps in Emily's old room, you know—it looks out over the garden."

"I know."

"It seemed as though that reflecting ball was shining into her room, somehow. And yet, how *could* it have been? There was no moon. But I saw it—I *did!*"

"Emily's reflecting ball," he said. "What else?"

"Oh, just little things. Jane says she sees Emily's face in the ball when she looks into it. And she wrote a poem—a little verse about the pansies—and she said that after she had been looking into the ball she 'just knew it,' and it was exactly—word for word—*exactly* like one Emily had written. Mrs. Canfield showed it to me in a notebook she kept."

"Jane had undoubtedly seen the notebook and something made her remember the poem."

"That's what I tell myself. But she *swears* she hadn't!"

"Louisa. Jane is an imaginative child, and right now she is living in a house where another little girl died. A little girl related to her. She is sleeping in that other child's room, playing with her toys, walking in the same garden, eating at the same table. Doesn't it seem rather natural that under these conditions a child like Jane might very well become overimaginative?"

"But *I* saw that light in her room, and the poem *was* the same! She didn't imagine those."

"When there is a logical explanation, Louisa, take it. The light was some odd reflection, perhaps of a downstairs light shining out onto the ball in the garden. The poem—she *must* have seen that notebook! It could have been some time ago, even before her parents died. Things one reads or hears can lie forgotten in the brain for long periods, and then be suddenly brought to light."

"I know it must be that way," I said doubtfully.

"Of course it is!" He rose from his chair. "Come along. Let's go outside and look at the water for a while before it gets dark."

We went out onto the wide veranda that circled the restaurant, strolled down the steps and wandered along a narrow boardwalk across the sand. The sky was filled with the dusky brilliance of sunset, and the water gleamed in deep rose and gold. We stood at the end of the boardwalk, breathing in the salty smell, feeling the soft warm breeze against our faces. Our hands were loosely linked.

"Adam," I said, "you don't believe any of what I told you, do you?"

His voice was thoughtful. "I'm a doctor, Louisa, and medicine is a science. I suppose I think like a scientist—in fact, rather than in fancy. But as a doctor I know something else. I have seen men die when all my knowledge told me they would recover, and I have seen the reverse happen as well. I watched a man once—I expected each breath he drew would be his last. His wife was there, in the hospital, and she sat beside his bed, holding his two hands. She would not let them go. She kept talking to him—softly, just murmuring —and she held his hands so tightly that her own were white. She stayed there the whole night through. I told her to go and rest, that I would call her, but she refused to leave. 'He will die if I let go of him, Doctor,' she said, 'and I am not going to let him die.' The man's pulse was so faint I could barely find it. Respiration was almost nonexistent. I *knew* he could not live. And his wife leaned closer and she called him—over and over she called his name—and she never let go of his hands. Sometime—in the dark hours of the morning—he opened his eyes, and he looked at her, and he said, 'Don't let go.' 'I won't,' she said. By the time it was light outdoors his pulse was firm, his breathing was normal, and he was sleeping restfully."

"And he got well?"

"He got well."

"Oh, Adam, that's beautiful!"

"Yes, it is. But it's more than that. It is one of the strange things that teach doctors how much they don't know." He looked down at me, and the softness of night crept across the water. "There is one thing this doctor does know, however," he said. "He is very glad you agreed to come tonight."

I looked up at him, determined to know. "Did Mrs. Canfield tell you to ask me?"

There was utter amazement on his face. "Did *what*?" He took a deep breath. "Look here, Louisa Amory! I'm a big boy now! I don't need anyone to make decisions for me."

"Then she didn't. I'm sorry. I mean—I'm sorry I thought she might have. I'm *glad* she didn't!"

"For a very pretty girl you get some strange ideas," he said. Then he pulled my hand through his arm. "Come on. Let's walk down the beach a ways. And we are not going to talk about anyone or anything but *you!* Understand?"

"Yes, Doctor," I said obediently.

"And one more thing! Tonight I am not a doctor. Tonight I am Adam Frost, who is having a *dandy* time, thank you!"

It was really a very nice evening!

# EIGHT

Although it was not very late when we came home
the house was dark downstairs except for a soft
light in the hall. Adam unlocked the door with my
key, and as I stepped inside he caught my arm
gently.

"Again soon, Louisa?" he asked softly. I nodded.

He put one hand under my chin and tipped my
face up and for a minute I thought he was going to
kiss me. Rather disappointingly he didn't. "Thank
you for coming," he said. Then he laid his cheek
against my hair. "You *smell* so good! All girl!"

He left and I closed the door after him. Feeling
quietly happy, I slipped the bolt into place, turned
out the light and went up the stairs, my way illumi-
nated dimly by another light in the upstairs hall.

As I went down the corridor I saw that Mrs.
Canfield's door was slightly ajar, and remembered
that she had asked me to let her know when I came
home. I knocked.

"Come in, Louisa," she said.

She was sitting up in bed, reading. As I entered
she laid her book face down on her lap and took
off her spectacles. In the soft light from the bedside
lamp her face looked gentle and serene.

"I just wanted to tell you I'm home, Mrs. Canfield," I said.

"Did you have a pleasant time, child? Adam is good company, isn't he?"

"Oh, yes! We had a lovely evening! Dinner, and a walk along the water—"

"Come and sit down for a moment and tell me about it. Unless you are very tired?"

"I'm not a bit tired!"

"Then stay a few minutes." She patted the edge of the bed, and I sat down, leaning back against one of the tall carved posts. We were both silent for a few seconds. Then, feeling that I had to know more, I said, "Mrs. Canfield, Adam talked about Emily tonight. I asked him to. He told me how she died."

"Oh?" Her tone made me wonder if I should have said it.

"The pneumonia," I persisted. "How she sat by the open window, wet to the skin—"

"Yes."

"It seems so incredible! Do you think she really knew what she was doing?"

"I'm sure she knew," Mrs. Canfield said quietly. "Whatever Emily happened to want she set herself to get, by one means or another. If I had been firm with her, if I had stood up against her whims, I could have disciplined her. And if I had, Louisa, I would have lost my husband's love completely. You may be too young to understand how much people will do—or leave undone—for love." She paused, then went on sadly, "I suppose the truth of it is that Emily and I both loved her father more than we did each other. Even for my daughter I could not displease my husband. And my daughter knew it."

"Adam says he feels it was his fault, in a way, that Emily died. If he had stayed with her—"

"Nonsense! I have always known that I . . . that if I had gone to Emily sooner it would not have happened. I knew the way her mind worked. I should never have supposed she would give in so gracefully. But it is easy to delude oneself, to believe what one wishes to believe." She sighed, and then added softly, "It is a terrible knowledge to live with, Louisa."

I leaned forward, laid my hand over hers. "Mrs. Canfield, I didn't mean to make you remember all these things. I'm so sorry!"

"It is not a case of remembering, child. One never forgets. One simply covers them up, hides them somewhere, builds a wall so they cannot be discovered. But since Jane has been here—well, I find that wall is not so strong. Jane has a way of getting through. I have become very fond of her, Louisa."

"It is because of Jane that I wanted to know about Emily. Jane seems . . . *obsessed* with her!"

Her dark eyes searched my face. "*Obsessed?*"

"She talks so much of her—she says she sees her face in the reflecting ball. And the other night . . ." I went on to tell her about the night that the ball sent the strange glow into Jane's room, and how I was at a loss to explain it.

There was a long moment's silence before Mrs. Canfield spoke again. When she did, it seemed to have no connection with what I had been saying.

"When Mr. Canfield died he was sitting in Emily's room, beside her empty bed. He often sat there. He . . . apparently had a heart attack. I heard him cry out his daughter's name. By the time I reached him he was lying across the bed. He must have died instantly."

"I don't understand," I said.

"And no one has ever been able to explain what could have made John's old horse bolt with the buggy that day. Never, *never* had it happened before. I think of these things, Louisa, and I remember how strong, how determined, how *ruthless* Emily was."

"Ruthless?"

"She wanted her own way. She did not like being alone. She wanted *her* people, *her* possessions, and *her* way. Always."

Suddenly I felt very cold and tired. My voice was hardly more than a whisper. "Mrs. Canfield. Are you saying that you think Emily is . . . is still getting her own way? You said she loved her father and her brother. That she liked to have them with her."

"So she did."

"Do you truly believe that she—"

"That in some way she 'took' John and her father to be with her? How can one ever know, Louisa? How can one ever know?"

I rose from the bed, feeling exhausted. "I'm sorry I mentioned these things, Mrs. Canfield. I should never have bothered you with Jane's . . . imaginings."

"Oh, yes, you should have. It is something I need to know about. Go to bed now, child. Go to bed and just remember the pleasant evening you have had. Good night, Louisa."

"Good night, Mrs. Canfield."

"And Louisa—don't fret."

I closed her door quietly and walked slowly down the hall to my room. For some reason I did not want the bright overhead light on. Rather than touch the wall switch I groped on the dresser for the candle and matches that were always there

in case the electricity should fail. The candle flame
reflected in the mirror that hung over the dresser,
a small flickering light that showed me my own
face, and—suddenly I gasped and pressed my
hand hard upon my mouth to stifle a scream.

Behind me, looking over my shoulder, dim in
the shadowy room, was another face—a face so
contorted with hatred that I could feel the prickling
of my hair against my scalp. Dark eyes glared into
mine in the glass, lips were drawn back over teeth
in a snarling grimace, black hair caught loosely
from the face on either side, falling in long curls
—Emily! I whirled, my back pressed hard against
the edge of the dresser. There was no evil figure
there, but the face remained. The face—a picture
propped against my pillow—a picture Jane must
have drawn, using charcoal for those dark, smol-
dering eyes, those clustered curls. It took all my
strength to walk across the floor, to lift the hateful
thing in my hand, to look at it closely. I switched
on the light then—the more light the better!—and
I could see it clearly. The childish way the corkscrew ringlets had been drawn, the clumsiness of
the details, but the expression was there, the sheer
hate, the venom—and something more too. Across
one corner, exact and beautifully formed, was the
signature "Emily Canfield." I knew beyond any
possible doubt that if I were to compare it with
something Emily had signed herself, there would
not be a shred of difference.

My fright and shock were now changing to
anger. I whipped into Jane's room, snapping on
the light. She slept deeply, lying comfortably
spread-eagled beneath the sheet, her hair spilling
across her face in a dark cloud. Mercilessly I shook
her.

"Jane! Jane, wake up this minute! Do you hear me? Wake up!"

She burrowed her head deeper into her arm. "Wake up, Jane! Now!"

Coming suddenly from sleep, she squinted her eyes against the brilliant light.

"Louisa! What is it? Is the house on fire?"

"You know what it is," I said, my voice low and filled with fury. "You drew that picture of Emily, didn't you? And left it on my bed to frighten me!"

"To *frighten* you? Oh, Louisa! Why would it frighten you? I never meant to do that! I just thought you'd like to see it."

"And the signature in the corner! The writing that says 'Emily Canfield.' Where did you copy that from?"

"I didn't copy anything from anything! I was just drawing a little before I went to sleep—Grandmother said it was all right—and I drew a picture of Emily, and it came out looking mad—because you were out with Dr. Frost, I guess—and I thought it was sort of funny. I thought you'd think it was funny, too. So I left it where you'd find it."

"What about the signature?" I repeated, stressing every word.

"The signature? I don't know. I just wrote down who it was, that's all."

"But that's not your writing, Jane. You copied it from somewhere, and I want to know where!"

Jane stared at me a moment, her lip quivering, and then she burst into tears. "Don't talk hard to me, Louisa! I never heard you talk like that before! You frighten me!" She reached out both arms to put them about my neck, but I caught her wrists and held her.

"Jane, where did you copy that signature from?"

"I didn't copy it, Louisa! I just . . ." She was sobbing so she could barely speak. "I just held the pencil and it came out that way! *Please* don't be angry!"

I let go her wrists and held her close to me, smoothing her hair and murmuring to her. "I'm sorry, Jane. Oh, Jane, I'm *so* sorry! I shouldn't have spoken to you like that. It was just—oh, never mind! It's all right, darling, truly it is! Everything is all right!"

I held her until her sobbing stopped, and then I straightened her bed and made her comfortable again before I kissed her good night. Hating myself for what I had done to her, for the fear and anger and lack of control I had shown, I went slowly back into my room. As I passed her window I looked out on the sleeping garden.

Below me the reflecting ball glowed lucent.

# NINE

I was pulled from a dark, fretful, heavy sleep the next morning by the feeling of a weight across my legs that kept me from moving. In quick panic I thrust one leg sideways as hard as I could. The weight was suddenly gone, there was a thud and someone said, "Ow!" I opened my eyes. Jane was sitting on the floor in her nightgown, looking at me reproachfully.

"You're still mad at me," she said, climbing back up on the bed.

"Mad at you? Why should I be mad at you?"

Then it all flooded back, the shock when I had seen the drawing of Emily, so alive and threatening in the shadowy room, the further shock and then the anger when I had seen that exquisite signature. I felt again the shame of losing my temper with Jane.

"Oh, Jane, darling! I'm not mad. I told you last night I was sorry. Don't you remember?"

"I wasn't sure. Well, that's all right, then! So now, tell me about last night. Was it nicer than you thought it would be?"

The pleasure of the evening before came back to me, and I smiled in spite of myself.

Jane crowed with delight. "It was! I can tell! Oh, I'm glad!"

"I'm glad you're glad."

"And you *like* him a lot better, too, don't you? Well, *that's* certainly a relief!"

I burrowed my face in the pillow to hide my silly grin. "Jane, you're impossible!"

"No, I'm not. You love me." She slithered off my bed and started into her room. As she passed my dresser she paused, and then picked up that horrible sketch. She stood studying it for a moment. "She's not very pretty in this picture. She was pretty in the picture Grandmother showed me, but not here."

"What picture did your grandmother show you?"

"It's in that black locket thing she wears. The one with the diamond or something stuck in the front of it. The back is a picture of Emily. Grandfather Canfield gave it to her when Emily died."

"I see."

"I thought I'd draw her the way she looked in the locket picture, but it didn't come out that way. It kept getting madder and madder while I drew." She laid the sketch carefully back on my dresser. "Emily doesn't let me draw her the way I want to. I don't think I'll try anymore."

"That's a very good idea," I said, slowly sitting up in bed. "In fact, I just wish you'd stop even *thinking* about her."

"I don't *mean* to think about her, she just comes popping into my head sometimes. And then I can't make her go away."

"When does she 'pop' into your head, Jane?" I sat on the edge of the bed. "Any special times?"

"Not really special. When everything is sort of quiet, I guess. When I'm a little sleepy, or when there isn't anybody to talk to, or when I'm in the garden—near that silvery ball thing. Mostly then. She kind of . . . lives in there."

"Oh, Jane, you know that's ridiculous!"

"Is it?" She looked up at me, her long hair loose around her face. "Well, she looks *out* of there quite a lot. Maybe she isn't *in* there, but she still looks out."

"Jane, I've tried to tell you! That's your own reflection—just distorted because the ball is round. You only *imagine* that it looks like Emily!" I could hear my voice rising. Jane looked at me thoughtfully and then turned and went into her room where she started to dress. Fuming, I began to put my own clothes on. A few moments later, half-dressed, I went to the connecting door. Jane sat on the floor, buckling her sandals.

"Jane," I said, trying desperately to sound calm. "Were you in the garden last night before you went to bed?"

She glanced up at me. "Yes. Grandmother and I went outside after supper."

"And did you look in the reflecting ball?"

"Yes. I always look in it when I'm outside, just to see if Emily's in there. She isn't always, you know. Sometimes it's only me." She looked down at the shoe as she slipped the strap through the buckle and added quickly, "And no matter *what* you say, Louisa, it isn't *always* me!"

I snatched a dress from my closet and put it on over my head, pulling it down into place with little angry tugs. I fastened the belt and went back into Jane's room.

"Come here and let me do your braids."

Silently she rose from the floor and stood with her back to me so that I could draw the brush through her hair. I could feel myself being a little rougher than necessary, but she said nothing. At last I burst out, "I'm going to ask your grand- mother to have that silly ball put away!"

Jane's hair jerked from the brush as she turned and looked up at me. "Oh, no, Louisa! We mustn't do that! It's Emily's special ball. She'd *never* for- give us if we took it away!"

I took her shoulders and held them tightly, leaning down to her. "Jane, I really couldn't care less about Emily! It's *you* I care about! She is dead! Do you understand? *Dead!* She was a spoiled, undisciplined, unkind little girl when she lived, and now she no longer lives. And whatever is done to that reflecting ball in the garden can make no difference to her now!"

Jane's eyes held mine. "That's not true, Louisa. And you know it isn't true. That ball belongs to Emily—it *still* does—and it would be dreadful to move it! Promise me you won't!"

"I will *not* promise! If you are going to upset yourself constantly with the thing, *I* am going to ask that it be moved!"

Great tears sprang to her eyes. "Please, Louisa, please don't! I'll stay away from it if you want. I won't go near the ball! But it's Emily's, and she has to have it there. Right there, where it is! It's the only way she can get through!"

"And that's precisely why I'm going to have it moved." I could feel my hands shaking as I gripped Jane's shoulders. "Because it's the only way she can get through!"

Jane stepped back, pulling herself gently from my grasp. Her eyes were dry now, but the tears had left streaks on her face. "You see, Louisa?" she said, and her voice was little more than a whisper. "You see? It isn't just me. *You* believe in

Emily, too. And you *must not move that ball!*"
Going to the door that led to the hall, she opened
it and stood looking back at me. A wistful, almost
sad, little smile touched her mouth. "Don't be
frightened, Louisa. Leave the ball alone. I'll try
not to go near it again."

She closed the door quietly behind her and
went off down the hall. I recalled then that I had
not braided her hair, but I felt too weak to call
her back.

# TEN

Something threatening seemed to hang over those hot, still July days. I was enjoying Adam's company, and should have been happy, but instead I was restless and uneasy, I found it difficult to settle down to needlework or reading, I preferred being with other people, rather than alone. I would often seek out Mrs. Canfield in her favorite spot under the tulip tree, and urge her to talk. One day I found the courage to ask her something that had puzzled me since that first evening when Adam came to supper.

"You talked about some lion, and some doors, I remember. I know I am ignorant, and I apologize, but it has bothered me ever since."

For a moment she looked baffled, then suddenly she smiled. "I remember now! The Lion of Lucerne. And it must have been Ghiberti's Doors, on the Basilica di San Giovanni in Florence. Poor Louisa! Why didn't you ask us then?"

"I felt so stupid!"

"It isn't stupidity, child. There is no real reason why you should know about them."

And she told me, about the beautiful golden doors, the Gates of Paradise, on which Lorenzo Ghiberti spent fifty years of his life, depicting scenes from the Old and New Testaments with such skill and artistry that now, five hundred years later, they remained among the most exquisite portals in the world. About the tragic Lion, carved in the living rock, commemorating the seven hundred brave Swiss guards and their officers who were killed trying to defend Louis XVI and Marie Antoinette when the Paris mob stormed Versailles.

"Oh, I wish I could see these things," I said. "There is so *much* I haven't seen!"

"But there is time. You are very young, my dear."

On my next trip to the library I came home with an armful of travel books which made Jane break into an exasperating chant.

"I know why you're reading those, I know why you're reading those! You want to impress the Doctor, you want to impress the Doctor!"

"I want to improve my mind," I said loftily.

"Fiddlesticks!" was Jane's only comment.

Only one thing seemed to lift the nameless shadow hanging over those days. When Adam's office hours were over he often turned his automobile into the driveway and came strolling round the corner of the house, knowing just where to find us. Jane generally joined us when she saw him arrive, and I was both amused and embarrassed by the open delight she took in any small gestures he might make toward me. If he touched my arm or my hand, or let his eyes rest on me while we talked, Jane's lips would curve into her smug I-told-you-so smile. Mrs. Canfield noticed the child's behavior too, and once remarked, "Jane, I believe you are an inveterate matchmaker!"

Adam laughed, but with such affection Jane could not be offended. "You are one of my favorite people, Jane!"

"Even more than Em——" she began, and then broke off short.

There was a moment's silence, and then Adam said softly, "Than Emily? It's all right if you don't *want* to talk about her, Jane. But don't keep it buttoned up inside if you *do* want to. That can cause trouble." Their eyes met. "Will you remember that?" he added.

"Yes," Jane said. "I'll remember."

As the hot days continued Jane played for hours with the dollhouse, moving the dolls from place to place and carrying on their conversations. She called the father and mother simply Mr. and Mrs. Doll, but to my delight the children were named Sonny, Honey, Flotsam, and Jetsam. When she was outdoors I noticed that she never went near the reflecting ball. If it happened to be in her path she would make a quick wide circuit of it and continue on her way without even a sideways glance. Nor did she mention Emily.

Letters continued to arrive from Martin, although not with their former regularity, but there were times when I almost forgot to open them. My constantly deepening interest in Adam had pushed poor Martin way to the back of my mind.

We found so much that we both enjoyed: evening walks, tennis games, drifting in a canoe where willow trees dipped their long fingers in the water. Everything we did together was a delight! And always we talked, each of us eager to learn everything about the other. Adam was formally invited to dinner on occasion, and other times Katie would come from the kitchen to say diffidently that "there looked to be a lot of meat on that chicken that was for dinner—if Dr. Adam would like to stay, that is."

Generally "Dr. Adam" was very happy to stay, though there were times when he had professional calls to make, or when he had records to go over with his father. On one such evening he refused the casual invitation regretfully, and I walked through the house with him and out onto the veranda as he prepared to leave.

The long last rays of the summer sun fell across the porch, shining full on Adam's face. As he had once before, he put his hand under my chin and lifted it, but this time I saw the deep, deep blue eyes come closer until I closed my own.

"Louisa," he said softly, and I felt his lips warm and firm and demanding on mine. I had never known before what a kiss could be! Far too soon he lifted his head, and I leaned mine against his shoulder.

"You never kissed me before," I murmured, probably the most ridiculous remark I ever made!

"But I will again," he said, and did. "And again, and again, and again!"

Weak and breathless, I tried feebly to push him away. "Adam! The sun is shining!"

He held me close, laughing softly. "Sunlight—moonlight—who cares?"

"People might see us!"

"Do you mind?"

"Jane might!"

"Jane has. With great interest. Look." He turned me slightly so that I could see the drawing room window that overlooked the veranda. From behind the stiff lace curtain two shining dark eyes peered out with delighted fascination.

"Ooh, that little—" I gasped, but Adam stopped me with one firm kiss.

"I love you, Louisa," he said. "I don't care if the whole world knows!" And before I could say another word he was down the steps. "I'll see you tomorrow," he called, and with my feet barely touching the floor I floated into the house.

Jane was still standing by the front window, and she faced me as I came in.

"I saw you," she said, as though she made an admission.

"I know," I said dreamily.

"Aren't you cross with me?"

"No."

"*Really*, Louisa?" She sounded unbelieving.

"Really, Jane. I'm not cross with you or anybody in the whole wide world. I love you! I love everybody!" My voice seemed to be caroling in the silliest way! "I'm going upstairs and lie down on my bed until I wake up. Because this *has* to be a dream!"

Jane looked at me and shook her head. "Golly!" she said. "I never thought love made people like this! Don't go to sleep, Louisa. It's almost time for dinner."

It was later that evening and Jane and I were playing a game of croquet on which I could not seem to keep my mind, when Katie called me from the back door.

"Dr. Adam's on the telephone, Miss Louisa. He wants to talk to you. He says it's very important and to hurry!"

I dropped my mallet and ran into the house and through the hall to the little table where the telephone stood. My heart was thudding. What could be so important? And why the hurry? I picked up the receiver.

"Hello? Adam? What is it?"

"I love you."

"Oh, I'm glad! I'm glad! But what is it that's so important? Why did I have to come so fast?"

"So I could tell you again that I love you. I couldn't wait any longer."

I stopped dead and then started to giggle. "Oh, Adam, you idiot! And here I thought something terrible must have happened!"

"What a gloomy mind you have! But I do have something else to say. Dad wants you to come to dinner tomorrow night. Here."

"Oh, heavens! Your *father*? Oh, Adam, I'm scared!"

"Now don't get edgy. You'll like him. Everybody does. You'll come?"

"All right," I said weakly.

"And Louisa . . . wear that white dress. The one you had on the first time I saw you. Please?"

"All right," I said again.

"Till tomorrow then. I'll pick you up at six. Good night, Louisa."

"Good night," I said, and hung up.

I sat there on the little bench by the telephone table for a moment, and then a board creaked farther along the hall, and I looked up. Jane stood in the far shadows.

"I wasn't listening, Louisa," she said instantly. "Honest! I didn't listen until you stopped talking."

"His father wants to meet me," I said shakily. "I'm going there to dinner tomorrow night."

"Oh, Louisa!" she breathed, coming closer. "That is a good sign! What are you going to wear?"

"A blanket. And I'll pull it over my head and hide inside it!"

She giggled. "He'll think you're an Indian. You could wear your white dress."

"Thank you. As a matter of fact I'm going to. Adam asked me . . . I mean—well, I guess he liked it."

"I knew he would. Louisa, is it all right if I tell Grandmother you're going to dinner?"

"I guess so. It's not a secret. Nothing *could* be, with you around!"

She ran back to me and hugged me violently. "Oh, Louisa, I do love you!" she said, and skipped off down the hall.

I went upstairs and while I waited for Jane I sat in the little armchair gazing out at the soft summer night. The faint light that remained seemed to have gathered in the silver of the reflecting ball, but now it was not ominous, only beautiful. I don't mind about you anymore, Emily Canfield, I said to myself. You no longer live, but I do! I can see now why you always wanted Adam with you, why you wanted to marry him when you grew up. But you never grew up. It's my turn now, Emily, and there's nothing you can do!

I heard Jane enter her room from the hall, and then her light shone through our connecting door.

"Grandmother says how nice you're going to dinner," she reported. "She says—" Jane's voice stopped suddenly. "Louisa, come here a minute, please."

I don't know what there was in her voice that chilled me even before I went into the room. "What is it, Jane?"

"Look." She pointed to the floor by the dollhouse. One of the dolls, one of the girl children, lay on the carpet, little chips from her broken china head scattered around her.

"Your doll! She must have fallen out of the dollhouse and smashed." I bent to pick it up.

"Smashed on the *rug*, Louisa? On the soft *rug*?"

"The wind, perhaps. Or Katie, cleaning. She must have brushed by the doll somehow, or perhaps it was already on the floor and she stepped on it."

"It wasn't on the floor. I put the dolls to bed before dinner. And Katie hasn't been up here since."

I gathered the tiny chips in my hand. "Well, *something* broke it, Jane. Maybe it was cracked before. It's quite old, you know."

"It wasn't cracked, Louisa."

I looked up at her, slightly vexed. "All right, then, *you* tell *me* how it broke!"

Her voice was no more than a whisper. "I don't know how. But I know who. Emily broke it."

"Oh, Jane!"

"Emily did it, Louisa. She doesn't like us having her things."

"What things?"

"The reflecting ball, and the dollhouse—and maybe Dr. Adam, too."

I got to my feet, took her gently by the shoulders and turned her toward me. "Jane, Emily could not have broken that doll. I don't know how it broke, but she couldn't have done it! She *couldn't* have! And you can't give her back the dollhouse, any more than I can give her back Adam. Emily's life is *over*, Jane! You *must* believe that!"

Jane took the doll and the tiny chips from my hand. "Poor Flotsam," she said. "I'll keep her somewhere safe. I don't want to throw her away."

I went back to my room while Jane undressed. When I looked out of the window again the garden slept in unbroken black. There was no light anywhere at all.

# ELEVEN

Jane spent most of the next morning trying to glue Flotsam's head together. She was not very successful.

"Why do you bother, dear?" I asked. "There are several other dolls."

She didn't look at me. "Somebody has to show her she can't always do just as she likes."

"Show who? *Flotsam?*"

"You know who."

Yes, I knew. And I didn't want to discuss it. Instead, I changed the subject.

"Oh, I wish dinner tonight were over with! Suppose Adam's father doesn't like me?"

"Grandmother says he's very nice! You mustn't be scared, Louisa."

"I'm not exactly *scared*—oh dear, yes I am too! I'm scared he'll think I'm just a frumpy country bumpkin! And I *am!*"

Jane was enchanted with the words. "Frumpy country bumpkin, frumpy country bumpkin," she kept repeating, until it finally came out "Frumpy cumpy crumpkin," which set her off into gales of laughter. It was the one bright spot in the day.

Adam had said he would call for me at six o'clock, but it couldn't have been more than four when I started to dress. I had spent the morning pressing every tiny ruffle on the white dress, so it looked as fresh as meadow daisies, but I agonized over whether to wear my tiny pearl earbobs, whether my white gloves would be too dressy, and what to do with my hair. It was not until I saw the approval in Adam's eyes that I was reassured.

The two Dr. Frosts lived in a rambling old house where they were tended with patient firmness by a tall, erect, soft-spoken Negro woman named Sarah. She greeted us in the hall when we arrived, and then Adam led me into a lovely large room, filled with beautiful old pieces of furniture, and lighted by the long shafts of early evening sunshine.

"Oh, Adam, it's charming!" I said. "Have you always lived here?"

"Always, and so did many Frosts before me." He stood tall and smiling, looking down at me. "I'm glad you like the house, Louisa. You look very right, standing in this room. As if you belonged here."

"Well, I'm glad I *look* right! I *feel* scared to death!"

"I know an excellent cure for that."

He kissed me slowly and deliberately, and my arms went tight around him and I wanted to be so close to him that nothing could ever, ever, ever come between us! I thought I heard footsteps, but I could not have moved if the roof had caved in on my head. Someone cleared his throat, Adam put me gently away from him, and I turned to see an older, burlier, grayer Adam standing in the doorway.

"Dad, this is Louisa Amory."

Dr. Frost came toward us, smiling. "Miss Amory," he said, taking my hand warmly in his.

"Do you know that ever since Adam told me you'd be dining with us tonight I have been in a state of panic?"

"*You?*" I said stupidly. "*I've* been in a dither all day, but why should you—"

"Being a father on display is unnerving. Sarah made me change when I came in; she all but inspected my fingernails and checked behind my ears before she would allow me to come downstairs."

I laughed, just as he had meant me to.

"I'm under an additional strain," Dr. Frost went on. "You see, you are the first girl my son has brought home since he was five. I knew this was something special."

I glanced at Adam, who was looking happily from one to the other of us like a little boy whose mother approves of his new playmate. He turned to his father.

"And now that you've seen her?" he asked.

"I don't know how you found her, Adam, but don't let her go!"

Dinner was delicious—Katie could have done no better—and Sarah, as she served it, beamed with pleasure. Later we returned to the drawing room where I managed to pour coffee without spilling a drop. As I passed Dr. Frost his cup he noticed me eyeing several bright little objects that hung from his watchchain.

"Those are my child-beguilers," he said, lifting the chain from the two pockets and handing it to me to look at. "It's almost as useful as my stethoscope."

There were some fraternal emblems and keys on the chain, and such other trinkets as a tiny gold whistle, a little doll with jointed limbs and jewelled eyes, a miniature harmonica, and a tiny enameled Easter egg with a scene inside.

"They distract the older children during my examination," Dr. Frost explained, "and the little ones find it excellent to cut teeth on."

"Completely unscientific," Adam said. "The American Medical Association would never approve!"

"More fools they." His father refastened the chain across his vest. "It was little Emily Canfield who first gave me the idea for that."

And suddenly I felt a chill in the room that had not been there before. I had forgotten Emily for hours, but now—as always—here she was again. My voice must have sounded strained, for Dr. Frost looked up at me quickly from under his shaggy brows when I spoke.

"Emily!" I said. "Always Emily!"

"You know about her, then."

"Oh, yes, I know about her. And I keep learning more all the time. How was she responsible for . . . what did you call them?"

"My child-beguilers. It was one of the many times Emily was ailing, or claimed to be. I put my stethoscope to her back and asked her to breathe deeply while I listened for congestion, but she flatly refused. This little gold whistle was on her bedtable, and I picked it up and admired it, and then asked her if she could blow it. When she blew, I listened. But I listened to her lungs, not to the whistle. It worked beautifully." He smiled, remembering.

"And didn't she realize what you were doing?"

"Not until it was too late. Then she was a